I hesitated at the front door. I had not been here for ten years. It felt wrong to just let myself in. It also felt wrong to knock at a door I had opened a million times. Without knocking.

I'd try the doorknob. If it was open, I'd let myself in. If it wasn't open, I'd knock and see if anyone came to the door. If no one came to the door, I'd try my key.

The door opened.

It was hard to imagine that there was still a place where people didn't keep their doors locked.

Going inside, I locked the door behind me.

Out of old habits, I went straight to the kitchen. My mother had always said the kitchen was the hub of the house and for her it was.

But at the moment, there was no one here.

There was a note on the counter. I flashed back to those days when I still lived here.

I stared at the note written in my mother's handwriting. The writing looked a little bit shakier than I remembered.

My parents had gone out.

To a movie.

They'd known I was coming in and not only had they not waited up, they had gone out.

When did my parents start going out?

And why didn't they just call or send a text?

Everything looked so much the same. I'd moved three times since I'd been home last time.

Three times.

And my parents lived in the same house they'd lived in my whole life.

Staring at the sparkling Christmas tree with some of the same ornaments they had on there when I was a child, I wondered what that might be like.

I needed to go out and get my luggage, but I decided to just sit down and rest for a few minutes. Check my messages and email.

Sitting on the couch, I pulled my feet up beneath me and got comfortable.

The fire in the fireplace had been banked. I thought about lighting it. Maybe open a bottle of wine and relax. Surely my parents had some wine around here.

"Oh good," a man said from behind me. "You let yourself in."

Startled, I sat up and looked toward the door.

A man in his late twenties at most, stood in the doorway smiling at me.

He was wearing jeans and a white button-down shirt beneath a long woolen sweater.

Clean-shaven. No ski mask.

He didn't look like a burglar.

And yet… I didn't recognize him.

"Yes," I said. "Of course."

"Come on back," he said.

Come back where exactly?

"I think I'll just stay here," I said.

IN A ONE HORSE OPEN SLEIGH

ALSO BY KATHRYN KALEIGH

Contemporary Romance
The Worthington Family

The Heart of Christmas

The Magic of Christmas

In a One Horse Open Sleigh

Second Chance Kisses

Second Chance Secrets

First Time Charm

Three Broken Rules

Second Chance Destiny

Unexpected Vows

Billionaire's Unexpected Landing

Billionaire's Accidental Girlfriend

Billionaire Fallen Angel

Begin Again

Love Again

Falling Again

Just Stay

Just Chance

Just Believe

Just Us

Just Once

Just Happened

Just Maybe

Just Pretend

Just Because

IN A ONE HORSE OPEN SLEIGH

THE WORTHINGTONS

KATHRYN KALEIGH

To learn more about Kathryn Kaleigh, visit

www.kathrynkaleigh.com

Kathryn Kaleigh

1

BELLA ALEXANDER

*H*olding a nice warm mug of hot coffee in my hands, I sat at the little round breakfast table in my condo's first floor kitchen and watched the fluffy white snowflakes drifting down, forming a layer of snow against the cold frosty glass.

A picturesque winter scene.

Not unusual for Pittsburgh. Not at all.

Yet for some reason it reminded me of home.

Whiskey Springs, Colorado.

Maybe it was because there were only four days until Christmas.

And for the first time in four years I was alone at Christmas.

I closed the lid on my computer and pushed it aside.

Whoever said teaching online classes was easier than teaching face to face did not know what they were talking about.

When I stood in front of a classroom, all I needed was my lecture notes. Maybe a PowerPoint.

But with online, I had to put my notes into modules.

Whoever came up with modules had far too much time on their hands. I know where it came from. It came straight out of the education department.

Psychology and education had always been at odds. Psychology was free and thought-provoking. Education was confined and restricted.

So I had to put my notes into online modules with three multiple choice questions at the end of each module and one essay question.

The essay questions were easy enough to generate, but they had to be graded and since online classes had high caps, each module could take hours to grade.

The heat kicked on, blowing warmth up from the floor out of the vent.

I held my hands out and shivered. It was funny how warmth, warm air... warm water... always made me shiver at first.

Sitting back again, I opened the box of cookies I had bought at the bakery and picking out a green tree-shaped sugar cookie, bit the top off the tree.

It tasted okay, a little dry, but it was nothing compared to the soft sugar cookies my mother made this time of year.

I glanced over at the big desk calendar laid flat on my dining table. I'd mapped out the Spring semester for all three of my classes. Physiological psychology. Counseling psychology. Psychology and movies.

I started my planning with the first day of classes in January, then finals weeks in May. Put in a date for midterms. That left two more exams. It wasn't that hard to do. Just paying attention to details.

But right now, all I could see was that tomorrow night was the tree festival in Whiskey Springs. The date was ingrained in my head.

And right about now, my mother would be starting to bake hundreds of cookies that she would donate to the festival.

For five years I had found one reason or another to not go home for Christmas. The last four years had been because of Anthony.

Anthony was a fellow professor whose family lived in Pittsburgh. He'd claimed his parents were getting older and he did not want to miss a Christmas with them.

He'd asked me to stay here with him.

And since I liked him, I had done just that.

But, damn it, my parents were getting older, too.

And Anthony was now dating the new girl we had brought in from California to teach the graduate students.

Anthony and I had been part of what I called the welcoming committee. We'd taken her... her name was Lisa... out to dinner when she had first moved here.

Then after we'd dropped her off, she'd called and asked Anthony to take a look at her door lock.

Since I was already getting ready for bed, Anthony had gone alone.

That had been the start of a downhill slide that led to them spending more and more time together.

She's lonely, he'd said.

Well I was lonely, too. And he had been *my* boyfriend.

I didn't let myself think about the sacrifices I had made. It just made me mad.

And I didn't have time for mad.

A flutter at the window caught my attention.

A bright red cardinal sat there on the window ledge, looking at me with brown eyes rimmed with black rings. His red feathers stood out against the white snowy backdrop.

We stared at each other for what must have been a good three minutes.

Then he fluttered off in a rush.

Well. I'd heard legends about cardinals at Christmas, but I had never actually seen one.

My heart racing, I reached for my phone and dialed my mother's number.

I closed my eyes while the phone rang.

Then it occurred to me, a bit belatedly, that it was only four o'clock in the morning in Whiskey Springs.

2

JACK FLEMING

*T*he office smelled like antiseptic.

I was, in fact, so used to the scent of antiseptic that I hardly even noticed it anymore.

And now was no exception.

When I opened the office door and stepped into the hallway, my senses were overwhelmed with the scent of baking cookies.

For just a moment, as I stood in the threshold between the office and the hallway of Doc Alexander's home, the scent of antiseptic and fresh baked cookies melded together into its own unique scent that I did not have a name for.

Mrs. Alexander was talking on the phone. I could hear her cheerful tone coming from the kitchen.

It was only five o'clock in the morning, but I was not only still on central time, I had trained myself a long time ago to get up early.

I was a proponent of early to bed and early to rise.

The habit had served me well. While my fellow med students were pulling all-nighters, I was up early, had my studies done, and in bed, usually by the time they started studying.

I'd learned that habit from my grandfather Noah Worthington. Grandpa had never steered me wrong. Just because I had gone to medical school instead of following him into aviation, didn't mean he wasn't my role model.

Ready for my second cup of coffee, but not wanting to interrupt Mrs. Alexander's phone call, I grabbed my large gray woolen coat and slipped out the back door.

With no more than a bare hint of daybreak, I used streetlights to guide my way toward town.

I walked toward the twinkling, colorful Christmas lights that draped everything that didn't move.

There was a little coffee shop I had been to several times on this side of town, within walking distance. There and back, in fact, would give me right at five thousand steps—one third of my daily goal.

Not a bad start to the day.

"Good morning," the young college student working as a barista standing behind the counter greeted cheerfully as I stepped through the door. She had been here yesterday, too. A chatty young lady who had asked me all sorts of personal questions, most which she hadn't given me time to answer.

Apparently I was the first customer today and the only one at the moment. I cringed, wondering what she was going to ask me today.

I was a rather private person, preferring to deflect attention away from myself and focus on others, usually the patient sitting in front of me. Most patients preferred it that way, in fact.

Unfortunately, I was granted zero latitude today.

"Mrs. Alexander came in yesterday," she said. "She said you're staying with them, in their guest quarters for a year while you do your internship."

Guest quarters might be a bit of an exaggeration. Guest room with its own private bathroom was more accurate, but I didn't bother to correct her. If Mrs. Alexander preferred for people to believe that she had a guest quarters in her home, then who was I to say differently?

A tall flocked Christmas tree stood in front of the window, its colorful, twinkling lights creating a cheerful mood, along with the strong scent of coffee, vanilla, and mocha. It was a real Christmas tree. A blue spruce with its distinctive scent.

The girl behind the counter began making my latte before I even told her what I wanted. Fortunately for her, I was a man of habit and always ordered the same thing. So I didn't say anything and it was just as well since she kept talking.

"A year is a long time to live with strangers," the girl said, turning on the frother. "But I guess after a year, they won't be strangers, will they?"

I just shrugged. Those were actually my thoughts exactly.

When I'd been matched with Doc Alexander in Whiskey Springs for my internship, I had not been happy. Whiskey Springs had been dead last on my list. Number eight. I had not told him that. Never would. Especially since he told me I was first on his list.

"Mrs. Alexander told me you don't have a specialty. At least not yet. You're more of a general practitioner."

When the girl paused and looked at me expectantly, I realized she was actually letting me answer.

"She's right," I said, getting a word in edgewise.

The girl grinned and slapped a lid on my coffee.

"Here you go," she said. "Enjoy."

"Thank you." I took my coffee and sat at one of the tables.

Normally I would walk on home, but the song playing through the coffee shop speakers was one of my favorites.

This was the first year I wouldn't be home for Christmas. Doc Alexander, a good man, had offered, but I didn't feel right sticking him with the Christmas shift. I was the intern, so I should be the one on call.

If it was something outside of my experience, he would be there, but for routine stuff, I needed to handle it. That was part of the commitment I had made to myself when I'd gone to medical school. I'd known that these first few years would be hard. That I would have to make sacrifices.

If I'd landed at one of the big hospitals in a city for my internship, I might have been happy to let those who lived local take Christmas day on call. But Doc Alexander was a one man team. Besides… and I had actually just learned this… he was practically retired.

I was his first and last intern.

Maybe he thought I'd like it here and stay. There was another doctor, who'd set up an office in town, but Doc didn't seem to think he'd be here for very long.

I watched the sun as it pushed away the darkness, reflecting off the snow-capped mountains.

Although Whiskey Springs was high in elevation, it was surrounded on three sides by tall, rugged snow-capped mountains.

The snow at the peaks was fresh, just fallen yesterday. Snow clouds had spent most of the day clustered around the peaks. A sure sign that it was snowing at the top.

Some people referred to the mountain tops as the high country, but as high in elevation as we were, I couldn't bring myself to think that Whiskey Springs was anything less than high country.

It was pretty country. I liked it that Whiskey Springs was just below the tree line. At every turn, there were aspens and blue spruce trees and firs.

The tree line was jagged, not clear like I would have expected.

But being born and raised in the flat world of Houston, I

was quickly learning about all sorts of mountain phenomena. Like when the clouds cluster around the mountain tops, it meant it was snowing up there. Who would have thought?

A whole lot different from what I was used to. I could spot hurricane clouds, but snow, not so much.

Two other men came inside the coffee shop while I sat there. The barista knew both of them by name and was chatty with them as well.

That was one thing about Whiskey Springs that I didn't know if I would ever get used to. How everyone knew everyone else and their business.

I was accustomed to the anonymity of the city. Probably why I preferred to keep my business to myself. It was what I knew.

In Houston, not too many people cared much about what other people did. I liked that. For me, a true conformist, I liked that it allowed people self-expression.

A paradox, I know.

But it wasn't for me to judge others. Only to try and heal them when I could.

Things were getting busy in the coffee shop, so I decided it was time for me to get back to the office.

Doc Alexander would be up by now.

3

BELLA

*B*y the time I neared Whiskey Springs, I had a very clear memory of just how much I could live without travel.

By the time I'd gotten to the airport, secured a flight, and reserved a rental car, I was having second thoughts.

But there came a point pretty quickly when there was no turning back.

I was going to Whiskey Springs.

The rental car's headlights illuminated the deserted highway as I followed the curvy mountainous road that opened up into town.

It always took my breath away to see the little town all lit up in the valley below. Especially at Christmastime. The whole downtown twinkled and glittered and sparkled in bright cheerful red and green mixed in with clear lights.

Five minutes later, I drove into Whiskey Springs, right down Main Street. With the radio off, I could hear the Christmas music blaring from the downtown speakers.

The shops would stay open late—at least eight o'clock—every night now until Christmas Eve. Families... couples... a few people who looked like they were in a hurry to get somewhere walked up and down the street.

Not too many were driving. Me excluded.

I drove through town until turning right onto Alexander Avenue.

My father's family had a long history here in Whiskey Springs. His father's father's... father's... father... I lost track of just how far back they went... was one of the founders of the town. He was also a doctor.

I found that rather baffling. That son after son followed their father's footsteps.

My brother and I were the end of that line.

My brother was an engineer and I was a psychology professor. No doctors in our generation. If either my brother or I didn't have children, we would literally be the end of the line.

And that made me sad.

I pulled into the driveway and parked.

The brightly lit Christmas tree twinkled from the living room window. The other lights were out.

I glanced at the clock on my dashboard. It was almost eight o'clock. It had taken me all day to get here.

And they hadn't even waited up.

It was okay. I'd asked them not to.

With Christmas just days away, this was a busy week for my family.

Whiskey Springs and Christmas were all but synonymous.

It wasn't that I had forgotten that. I just hadn't had any reason to focus on it lately.

A few stray snowflakes fell onto my windshield, melting immediately.

I turned off the motor and grabbed my handbag.

I'd come back out in a bit and get my two suitcases.

I opened the door to a blast of cold wind that nearly took my breath away.

I had to reacclimate myself to the high elevation. It was cold in Pittsburg, but it seemed colder here. Maybe it was just because I had been in a warm car for the past few hours.

I hesitated at the front door. I had not been here for ten years. It felt wrong to just let myself in. It also felt wrong to knock at a door I had opened a million times. Without knocking.

I'd try the doorknob. If it was open, I'd let myself in. If it wasn't open, I'd knock and see if anyone came to the door. If no one came to the door, I'd try my key.

The door opened.

It was hard to imagine that there was still a place where people didn't keep their doors locked.

Going inside, I locked the door behind me.

Out of old habits, I went straight to the kitchen. My mother had always said the kitchen was the hub of the house and for her it was.

But at the moment, there was no one here.

There was a note on the counter. I flashed back to those days when I still lived here.

I stared at the note written in my mother's handwriting. The writing looked a little bit shakier than I remembered.

My parents had gone out.

To a movie.

They'd known I was coming in and not only had they not waited up, they had gone out.

When did my parents start going out?

And why didn't they just call or send a text?

I laid my purse on the counter and went in search of water. Unable to find any water bottles in the refrigerator, I filled a glass with water from the sink and drank deeply.

I hadn't realized just how thirsty I was.

Putting the glass away, I wandered back toward the living room.

Everything looked so much the same. I'd moved three times since I'd been home last time.

Three times.

And my parents lived in the same house they'd lived in my whole life.

Staring at the sparkling Christmas tree with some of the same ornaments they had on there when I was a child, I wondered what that might be like.

I needed to go out and get my luggage, but I decided to just sit down and rest for a few minutes. Check my messages and email.

Sitting on the couch, I pulled my feet up beneath me and got comfortable.

The fire in the fireplace had been banked. I thought about lighting it. Maybe open a bottle of wine and relax. Surely my parents had some wine around here.

"Oh good," a man said from behind me. "You let yourself in."

Startled, I sat up and looked toward the door.

A man in his late twenties at most, stood in the doorway smiling at me.

He was wearing jeans and a white button-down shirt beneath a long woolen sweater.

Clean-shaven. No ski mask.

He didn't look like a burglar.

And yet… I didn't recognize him.

"Yes," I said. "Of course."

"Come on back," he said.

Come back where exactly?

"I think I'll just stay here," I said.

4

———

JACK

I'd left the door unlocked, just as Doc Alexander had instructed. He assured me that my appointment would let herself in.

My patient, her name was Jenny, had called for a late appointment. She'd taken the day off and said the day of rest hadn't helped any.

She was still feeling under the weather.

Since Whiskey Springs had no hospital and no trauma unit, this was about as close as a person could get to emergency care without driving into Boulder. And if a person wasn't feeling well, they certainly didn't need to be doing that.

I'd sat in the office, reading the latest medical journal while I waited. I'd quickly lost track of time.

I still wasn't used to walking out of the office into someone's living room. I suppose by the time I left here, it would seem normal.

I wasn't sure if that was a good thing or not.

There was no fire burning in the fireplace right now, but there were four stockings hanging from the mantle. Each one had a name embroidered on it.

Mom. Dad. Bella. Charlie.

The stockings seemed a bit forlorn to me. Maybe because there were no presents in them. And for that matter, there were no presents under the Christmas tree.

The tree twinkled and sparkled and as always left me feeling nostalgic for home.

I would get past this Christmas in Whiskey Springs and keep moving forward. This year would pass. A blip on my radar.

After this year, I would be able to make it a point to be home for Christmas.

I made a quick assessment of the young lady sitting on the sofa. She looked quite comfortable. Her feet tucked up beneath her in that way that girls had a tendency to sit. With two sisters, a host of cousins, and aunts, I knew these things.

Her dark brunette hair was stylishly cut, framing her face nicely with a chin length in front and coming to a long point in back.

I had two initial impressions. Well, three. The first one didn't necessarily count because it was purely visceral.

She was what my grandpa would call a *looker*.

My second impression was that she did not look exactly like she was from Whiskey Springs. I couldn't say why exactly I had that impression, but there was something about her. Maybe later I would sort out that thought and make sense of it.

My third impression was strictly medical. She looked tired.

"I think I'll just stay here," she said, looking at me warily.

"Not a problem," I said, going to sit next to her on the sofa, pulling a thermometer out of my sweater pocket.

She looked at me like I had lost my mind as I held it up to her forehead.

"What are you—?" She pulled away from me.

"No fever," I said. I checked her lymph nodes beneath her jaw line.

Then I pulled my stethoscope from around my neck.

By the time I had the thing in my ears, she was standing up.

"What are you doing?" she asked.

"An exam," I said. I didn't have any history on Jenny. Maybe she was a psychiatric patient.

"Who are you?"

I just looked at her. As I tried to formulate an answer, she took another step back.

"I'm Doctor Jack Fleming," I said, at a loss as to what else to say.

"What are you doing?" she asked again.

"You said you weren't feeling well, so I was examining you. For illness." I added lamely.

She laughed. Sort of a laugh. More of a scoff really.

"Who. Are. You." She said the words slowly as though I was having trouble understanding English.

I took the stethoscope out of my ears and looped it back around my neck.

Maybe I needed to start at the beginning.

"My name is Doctor Jack Fleming. I'm interning here with Doc Alexander." I stopped. Took a breath. I couldn't interpret her expression. "He's not here tonight, so I'm filling in for him right now."

"Intern," she said.

"Yes. Intern."

"From?"

"I'm from Houston," I said, not really knowing what kind of answer she was looking for. My hometown... My university...

She sat down hard in a chair across from me, looking at me with her head tilted to one side.

It was so quiet, I could actually hear the ticking of the grandfather clock in the foyer.

I was at a loss.

"You called," I said. "And made an appointment, right?"

She didn't answer.

Someone knocked on the door.

Jenny and I looked at each other.

The person knocked again.

Jenny and I both moved toward the door at the same time.

5
_____

BELLA

*C*old air, with a few flurries of soft snowflakes, swept inside as I opened the front door.

A young lady, her nose red, stood on the other side of the door, huddled in a gray woolen peacoat.

Being the daughter of a physician who had patients regularly coming to our home, I immediately decided that she was here to see a doctor.

I was fairly certain that it wasn't just the cold making her nose red. Her eyes had that glazed look that came with a bad cold.

I was keenly aware that the man... Doctor Fleming... stood behind me.

The girl looked at me, then looked over my shoulder at him. Whoever this Doctor Fleming was, she looked at him with recognition.

If everything in the house—the stockings over the fireplace, the note from my mother—hadn't looked so familiar, I would have thought I was in the wrong house.

"I'm here to see Dr. Fleming," the girl said.

"I'm Dr. Fleming," he said, but I didn't move.

The girl sniffled and I realized she was utterly miserable and I was keeping her standing outside in the cold.

So I stepped aside.

"Please," Doctor Fleming said. "Come in."

The girl glanced at me warily and came inside.

"Come on back," Doctor Fleming—Jack—said.

The girl followed him back toward the office.

Toward my father's office.

I closed the door and after staring at it for a moment, locked it, although I wasn't quite sure if there was any need to lock the door at this point. There were so many strangers in my parents' house that it seemed counterintuitive to lock the door with me on this side of it.

Utterly confused, I went into the living room and sat back down.

The girl recognized Jack, but she didn't recognize me. And it was *my* parents' home.

I stared at my phone. Halfheartedly glanced back at my recent text messages from my father. Then my mother. Then the thread with all three of us on it. But I was certain neither one of them had mentioned an intern named Jack staying in the house.

Sitting back in the chair, I stared at the cold fireplace. Someone, probably my father had laid a fire in the firebox.

I got up, found a lighter and held the flame against the kindling until it caught. Kneeling on the slightly threadbare rug, I sat back on my heels as the flames moved from the kindling to the logs, growing in strength as it went.

It had been awhile since I'd smelled real wood burning. I held my hands out to the heat and stared into the flames.

There was something fundamentally wrong with this whole situation.

It told me that it had been entirely too long since I had been home.

And it also told me that there was more of a distance between me and my family than I had realized.

My mother hung our stockings up every year. She always told me that.

But neither my brother nor I had had the decency to show up for a number of years.

My brother had come home last Christmas, but I took a selfish solace in him not being here now.

Somehow the two of us had used each other to justify not coming home.

Our parents should have said something.

But that wasn't fair.

They wanted us to have our own lives. To be independent. They had both said so countless times.

But having family came with responsibilities and no matter what my brother did, I knew I had neglected my duties as a daughter.

And yet I was here and they weren't.

I blew out a breath and went back to my chair.

I needed to bring my luggage in before it got any colder.

Then I was going to find that glass of wine.

6

JACK

*F*orty-five minutes later I let Jenny out the front door with an admonition to go straight home—she had walked, of all things—take her antibiotics and go to bed.

Rogue snowflakes were falling. Not a full blown snowstorm yet. But it was cold.

Doc Alexander's suggestion that I wear a woolen sweater instead of a lab coat had been spot on.

Even inside the old house, it was chilly.

Besides, a lab coat was too formal for this setting.

I closed the door and locked it, but not before taking note of the late model sedan sitting in the driveway.

It reminded me that I had another problem to deal with.

Since Jenny had walked, the car obviously belonged to the *looker.*

My hands in my pockets, I wandered back to the living room, fully expecting to see her there.

But the living room was empty.

She had lit the fire, but she wasn't here now.

I checked the kitchen, but she wasn't there either.

Since that had to be her car, I could only surmise that she had gone upstairs to one of the rooms.

I turned on the hot water pitcher to make a cup of tea.

I knew that the Alexanders had two adult children and I was pretty sure their names were Bella and Charlie.

Other than that, I knew very little about them.

I put a tea bag in a mug and leaned against the counter.

Doc Alexander talked to me mostly about the practice, of course. He'd already taught me a lot about what it was like to own a small practice in a small town. He loved it. That much was evident.

I could see it in everything he did. The way he talked it. The way he interacted with patients. From reading his notes. He almost always included a little something personal listed in each person's chart that he could talk to them about when they came in. Something to give them the feeling that he cared about them personally. And I believed that he did.

Mrs. Alexander was also most welcoming and friendly. We talked a lot, but mostly we just talked about general things like the weather. She was the one who had explained about the snow clouds clustering on the mountain peaks.

She talked to me about Whiskey Springs and its Christmas traditions. As a result, I knew that tomorrow night was the Tree Decorating Festival. A contest really. Afterwards, the trees were auctioned for charities. Which reminded me that I was supposed to go and help her decorate a tree. I think she had chosen a medical theme for her tree. Wasn't sure exactly what that meant, but I knew that whatever she had up her sleeve, it would be worthy.

The next night was more for children. A narrow-gauge train ride around the city. Then the next night, Christmas Eve was, oddly enough, a dance.

I found it odd that the town came together on Christmas Eve.

In Houston, everything closed down by Christmas Eve and by then people were doing their own things.

I filled my mug with hot water, added a little honey, and wandered back to the living room.

I stood in front of the fireplace, warming my hands on the warm mug and staring into the flames.

I'd already charted my appointment with Jenny, so everything I needed to do for tonight was done.

Doc and Mrs. Alexander had gone out to see a movie.

Mrs. Alexander had confided in me that they hadn't done anything together like that in ages, but since Doc had made the decision to start the retirement process, he had been more relaxed.

I was happy for them.

Another reason I didn't mind staying over the holidays and covering any appointments that might come up.

"When did my father take on an intern?"

As I turned and faced *the looker*, several thoughts collided in my mind at the same time.

One, of course, was a little spurt of adrenaline that *the looker* was still here.

Second, *the looker* had to be none other than Bella Alexander, Doc's prodigal daughter returned.

And third, no one had bothered to tell me that she was coming. Not that they had to, but it would have been nice to not feel quite so hapless and caught off guard.

As it was, I just stood there staring blankly at who could be none other than Bella Alexander.

Not only had no one told me she was coming, no one had warned me that she was beautiful.

7

BELLA

*D*r. Jack Fleming stood in my spot in front of the fireplace.

In front of my fire, which was blazing quite well, if I did have to say so myself. I may not have laid it, but I had lit it and that should count for something.

The room was in shadows except for the fireplace and the twinkling tree lights.

Under other circumstances, I would have found it quite romantic.

But at the moment, I was too annoyed.

I was annoyed at my parents for not telling me they had hired an intern.

I was annoyed that he was standing in my spot.

And I was annoyed that the intern was so good looking.

I took my glass of red wine and sat on the sofa, pulling my feet up beneath me, pretending that I wasn't annoyed.

"A few weeks ago," he said. "They didn't tell you?"

I took a sip of my wine and tried to look past him into the flames. He was messing up my plans for a nice relaxing evening.

"No," I said. "They didn't tell me."

"Huh," he said.

I somehow refrained from rolling my eyes.

He obviously wasn't going to volunteer any details without me asking. I didn't feel like asking. I felt like relaxing. But he left me no choice.

"Are you living here?" I asked. It was the only explanation for why he was here this time of night.

I'd expected him to see his patient and go, but instead, he appeared to be making himself quite comfortable. Obviously not going anywhere.

"Yes," he said.

I lifted an eyebrow questioningly.

"In the guest room." He straightened and sipped from his mug.

"For how long?"

I found myself holding my breath, waiting for his answer, and that annoyed me, too.

Just because he was handsome did not mean that I needed him staying here through Christmas.

In fact, since this was my first time home in ten years, it seemed like my parents would have waited home for me.

Maybe if I had told them what time to expect me...

"A year," he said.

I looked up him, meeting his gaze. That was not the answer I had expected. My next questions were to ask him how far into his internship he was and if he was staying over Christmas or going home.

I felt confident that home for him was someplace else.

But instead, I got distracted by his smiling blue eyes.

He slowly lowered his mug and I saw that not only were his eyes smiling, but the corners of his mouth were tilted up as well.

Our gazes held for what I considered to be a couple of seconds too long.

Since I had a tendency to overthink things and was doubtless doing just that right now, I tugged my gaze away from his and sipped my wine.

He was annoying. Just plain annoying.

Didn't he see that he was blocking my warmth from the fire?

I stared past him, wanting him to move out of the way, but not willing to give him the satisfaction of saying anything.

"When do you expect my parents back?" I asked, mostly just to fill the silence. I shifted in my chair, making it a point to lean to the left to perhaps catch a little bit of warmth.

"They didn't say." He stood his ground and if I hadn't found it ridiculous, I would have sworn he was not moving on purpose.

He couldn't possibly know that he was being annoying. If he did, I was certain he would move aside. It was what any normal person would do.

But Jack, it seemed, was not a normal person.

He was one of those annoyingly handsome men who didn't have a care in the world about anyone other than himself.

Since my evening was ruined in so many ways, I leaned back in my chair and closed my eyes.

Breathe in. Breathe out.

Those of my profession swore that it would work.

Personally, I was not convinced.

8

JACK

*B*ella Alexander was fetchingly beautiful.

And for some reason, it appeared that I annoyed her.

I was fairly certain that she was especially annoyed by me standing in front of the fireplace, although I was also pretty sure that she was actually annoyed that I was here and she hadn't known it.

I didn't blame her.

If my father hired an intern to live in his home and didn't tell me, I would be upset, too.

That would never happen though. I had too many aunts and uncles. Too many siblings.

Someone would know and then suddenly everyone would know.

Our family was not known for keeping secrets from each other.

Some even suggested that we were enmeshed, whatever that meant. A family by nature was enmeshed.

If it wasn't enmeshed, it was estranged.

And if estranged looked anything like Bella, I would take enmeshed over estranged any day.

"You didn't tell them, did you?" I asked.

She opened her eyes and looked at me.

Her eyes were a lovely mossy green. One that I'd rarely seen before.

It was funny that I would be attracted to someone so annoyed with me.

I found myself wondering what she would look like if she actually smiled.

I couldn't imagine.

But I found that I very much wanted to know.

"Not really," she said, surprising me with the admission.

Something in her voice struck a chord with me and I stepped away from the fireplace, dropping into the chair opposite the one she was sitting in.

"Thank you," she said, keeping her expression blank.

"You're welcome." I said, biting the inside of my cheek to keep from outright grinning.

I had a feeling she would not find it amusing, nor would she appreciate me finding it amusing that I knew what she was thanking me for.

She narrowed her eyes at me, confirming my suspicions.

She couldn't hide it though. She was drawn to the flames.

I wanted to ask her why she hadn't told her parents she was coming home. I wanted to ask her why she hadn't been home for years.

But I probably wasn't supposed to know that. A child did not need strangers drawing attention to things they couldn't possibly be proud of. Besides, there was nothing she could do about it now.

And she was here now.

I was no psychologist, but I knew a thing or two about

people. I decided that what she needed right now was a bit of nonjudgmental companionship, so that's what I gave her.

"Got any more of that wine?" I asked after a few minutes of holding my cold mug. If I was going to hold something cold in my hands, it might as well be a glass of wine.

"Kitchen," she said, her gaze fluttering to mine.

She gazed at me from beneath dark, thick eyelashes framing those mesmerizing green eyes that seemed so intense it felt like she could see into my very soul.

Maybe it was better... safer... when she was looking annoyed.

The way she was looking at me right now was a little disconcerting to say the least.

"Dr. Fleming," she said.

"Jack." I said, automatically.

"Jack."

An awareness of her hit me in the stomach like a sucker punch.

I didn't know what it was about her, but there was something.

9

BELLA

"Jack?" I said again since he didn't appear to have heard me the first time.

One of the logs broke in two and fell apart sending little embers skittering up the chimney like fireflies.

"Yes?" He blinked, seeming to focus back on me.

"The wine," I said. "The wine is in the kitchen."

"Right," he said, but he made no effort to move.

I shrugged and leaned back again. I wasn't going to go get the wine for him, if that was what he was thinking.

Then I heard the garage door lumbering open, signaling my parents being home.

"They're back," Jack said.

"About time."

He smiled. "They'll be happy to see you."

"Maybe," I said with another little shrug.

I hadn't told them what time I would be here because I hadn't known.

Jack nodded toward the stockings hanging over the fireplace.

Seeing the stockings there gave me a nice shot of guilt.

"They'll be happy," he said.

"Will you be going home for Christmas?" I asked.

"I have to stay here," he said. "I'm on call."

On call. Had my father actually asked Jack to stay here and work through the holidays? Or was Jack like me, preferring to stay and work over going home to family?

Maybe he had a girlfriend here. That could explain a lot. That had been my excuse.

I was working out how to ask him that without being obvious when he stood up.

"I'm going to head up to my room," he said, standing up. "Give you some privacy."

"Oh," I said, also standing up. "You don't have to do that."

He looked at me curiously. "Not wanting to face them alone?"

"What?"

"If you need me to stay, I can. Just thought you might like some privacy."

"You don't have to stay for me," I said quickly. "Go ahead and get some sleep."

He smiled slowly. "See you tomorrow."

Then he turned and headed up the stairs.

I slowly blew out a breath as I tried to sort out what had just happened.

I didn't need him to stay with me as I greeted my parents, so that hadn't been it.

But I wanted him to stay.

I'd wanted him to stay because... I was attracted to him.

This was going to be an interesting Christmas.

A whole lot more interesting than I had expected.

I had come here to see my parents.

I hadn't come here to find a man I was attracted to.

I took a deep breath and walked toward the kitchen to see my parents.

I would have to worry about Jack Fleming later.

The later the better, in fact.

I did not have the time or the inclination to worry about him right now.

I was here to have a nice relaxing Christmas.

To visit with my parents and enjoy a few days away from my usual routine.

It was time to reconnect with my family.

That was all.

I would not worry about Jack Fleming.

10

JACK

As always I woke early the next morning.

I stretched and stared out my window. I had a habit of leaving the long velvet curtains open at night to let in the moonlight. The sun wasn't up yet. At least not on this side of the house. If I wanted to see the sun rise, I had to go to the opposite side of the house. I'd found that the balcony on the east side was the best place to watch the sun come up.

Back in Houston, I could simply wake up and look out the east side window of the bedroom of my twenty-sixth floor condo or I could walk around and sit at my breakfast table with a cup of coffee.

Either way, I had watched hundreds of sunrises over downtown Houston and I never tired of it. It never got old. It was like watching a work of art being created every day.

The sunsets were magnificent, too, but by the time sunset rolled around, I was usually busy somewhere else.

New place. New routines.

I rolled out of bed and went to the shower. Living in someone else's house, I couldn't just walk down to the kitchen for coffee or anything else in my sleep pants and t-shirt, no matter how early it was and how unlikely it was that anyone else was up.

So into the shower I went. I let the hot water spray over my head for at least five minutes longer than necessary.

It was a good way to start the day. I did my best thinking in the shower.

But today my thoughts were clouded with Bella Alexander.

I would see her again today.

And hopefully I would be able to keep my thoughts straight in my head.

No guarantee though.

I had to accept it. Accept that I found her attractive.

With any luck, it would pass. Physical attraction didn't always stand the test of time, after all. Did it?

But when Cupid's Arrow struck, it struck deep.

She was, in effect, the boss's daughter. Needed to leave that alone.

She didn't live here and neither did I. I didn't know where she lived, but it didn't matter. I was here for the next ten months and she was somewhere else.

When I got back to Houston, I would find a nice girl to fall in love with and have some kids.

It was what we Worthingtons did.

I was on a path.

A straight and narrow path. And I followed the rules.

Medicine and aviation both required rules. Without rules, lives could be lost.

Simple as that.

I turned off the water, dried off, and got into a pair of jeans and a t-shirt.

I didn't have any appointments scheduled today.

But I would be seeing Bella.

I looked through my closet, sliding hangers aside one by

one. Debated between a white button-down shirt and a sweatshirt.

I shrugged. It was cold. I'd start with the sweatshirt. I could always change later. Before Mrs. Alexander dragged me off to the Tree Festival.

Besides, Bella didn't look like the kind of girl who got up as early as I did. Not too many people did.

I firmly believed that early to bed made a man healthy, wealthy, and wise.

There just weren't that many of us willing to make the sacrifice.

I'd go insane if I had to lie in bed until eight o'clock. Half the day would be gone.

I pulled the sweatshirt on over my t-shirt and put on my hiking boots.

It was time to go find a sunrise.

And enjoy the best part of the day. My alone time.

When I opened the bedroom door, I walked right into the aroma of coffee and... bacon?

I shook my head. Surely I was imagining things.

11

BELLA

I normally ate a banana and maybe some yogurt for breakfast.

But my parents were old-fashioned. They still liked to start their days with bacon and eggs.

So since I was awake early anyway, I decided to surprise them with a big breakfast.

Besides, I was pleased with the cappuccino machine sitting on the counter. My gift to my parents. Delivered last night.

I'd ordered it before I even decided to come and visit. Maybe the visit and the coffee maker were somehow unconsciously connected, but that was too much for me to figure out right now.

At any rate, it was something of a splurge for me and I needed to practice with it so I could teach Momma and Daddy how to use it.

They were going to love it. Both of them, just like most people, liked their designer coffees.

Since I was on eastern time, it wasn't early for me.

I turned the bacon, and stood back, sipping my coffee.

The sun would be rising soon.

Already, dawn was breaking over the rugged mountain tops, the sun's soft pink glow reflecting off the new fallen snow.

I hoped it snowed for Christmas.

Didn't need to drive anywhere. Didn't have anyone coming in.

My brother was staying in Houston to spend Christmas with his fiancé's family this year. They were coming here for New Years. By then I'd already be back in Pittsburg.

My parents didn't seem to mind. They appeared to have adapted quite well to not having their adult children around.

Kind of sad. But kinda took the pressure off.

I didn't want to think of them sitting here wishing for their family to show up.

Maybe it would be different if they had grandchildren.

Maybe they would have made the effort to visit their children.

But with my dad being the primary physician in town, it was hard for him to get away.

Not so much anymore.

They hadn't talked about Jack.

We'd talk about him later.

We hadn't talked about much, actually. It had been late and we had all been ready to turn in.

"I thought I was the only one who got up this early."

I yelped and nearly spilled my coffee.

Jack stood behind me, already wearing blue jeans and a sweatshirt. His hair was damp and he smelled like a fresh shower.

I swallowed and forced my thoughts to stay on track.

"Well," I said, setting my mug safely on the counter and turning slightly to face him. "I'm on eastern time."

He nodded slowly. "I see."

"What's your excuse?" I asked, forcing myself not to think

about how good he smelled or how sexy his damp hair was as it curled against his neck.

He shrugged. "I'm an early riser."

I nodded and used the tongs to turn the bacon over again. It was crispy, so I began the process of taking it up to drain on a plate lined with paper towels. My hands trembled a bit with acute awareness that Jack had walked to the coffee machine and was standing only a few feet away.

His hands on his hips, he studied the coffee machine.

"Thinking about walking to the coffee shop to get a latte. You want one?"

I held up my coffee mug. "I'm good."

He nodded, but he made no move to leave. It occurred to me that he didn't know how to use the cappuccino machine.

I had tucked my parents' old coffee pot in the bottom cabinet.

"Why don't I make you a coffee?" I asked.

He hesitated. Then stuffed his hands in his pockets and shrugged.

"Sure," he said, a bit sheepishly.

I grinned.

I felt a little bit sorry for him. The guy didn't know how to use a cappuccino machine. He probably had a lot of student loans and was probably just scraping by.

I'd only used this machine once, but I was fairly confident that I could make a simple cappuccino.

Maybe it would have been easier if he hadn't been watching me so closely. It was a little disconcerting.

12

JACK

I had an automatic coffee machine in my condo—built in. But it was so completely different from the monstrosity sitting on the counter in front of me.

This thing had gauges and dials and pumps. And might require my brother-in-law, an actual engineer to figure out how to work it.

My coffee maker had a panel—with pictures—that allowed me to make a selection and push a button, giving me whatever expresso-based coffee—or hot chocolate or hot tea—that I might want.

Once a week, the housekeeper serviced it, adding milk and coffee beans and whatever flavors a person could want in their coffee.

For me, it was simple to use, allowing me to have my designer coffees in my own condo and I didn't have to learn how to work this industrial-looking thing that resembled something that belonged in the surgical room.

But as I watched Bella work the dials, I was impressed.

"Lots of foam?" she asked.

"Sure," I said. "Whatever is easy."

"It's not so bad," she said.

And then before I knew it, she was handing me a mug of coffee.

Not bad. Tasted as good as the coffee shop.

"I'm impressed," I said.

She smiled.

And I froze, the mug just inches away from my lips, all my thoughts scattered.

Now I knew.

She was *a looker* when she was annoyed.

When she smiled, she was stunningly beautiful.

Cupid's arrow hit me again, this time going all the way through my heart.

So much for my hope that I could keep my thoughts straight.

There was no hope for me now.

"I'm glad you like it," she said. "It's my Christmas gift to my parents."

"You set it up." Very odd. My family would have kept it in the box, wrapped it up, and set it under the tree.

"I know," she said. "It was rather selfish of me, wasn't it?" She picked up her own mug and sipped.

"What do you mean?"

"I mean my excuse is that I had to learn to use it so that I can teach them how."

"A valid excuse," I said. Did this mean she was leaving right after Christmas? "You don't have one at home?"

"Oh no. This would be too much of a splurge for me. I don't drink all that much coffee."

"I see."

"And in the meantime, I have good coffee while I'm here." She smiled again. "That's the selfish part."

"I'm sure they understand," I said, then put my cup to my lips to avoid having to say anything else. I almost told her that the coffee shop downtown had perfectly good coffee and was within easy walking distance. But she seemed to be very proud of her gift to her parents.

I glanced toward the window. "Thank you for the coffee." I paused. Gauged my position. Decided to go for it. "I was heading up to the second-floor balcony to watch the sunrise."

She glanced back at the pile of bacon and the bowl of eggs she was in the process of working on scrambling. "Would you like some breakfast?" she asked. "To take with you?"

It did smell good. "Sure," I said. "But... only on one condition."

"What's that?"

"Join me."

13

BELLA

When I had gotten up this morning, I had not expected to find myself having breakfast on the second-floor balcony of my parents' house.

It was all a rather strange twist of events that had gotten me here.

Although I was bundled up in my coat, it was cold.

And yet… it was worth it.

The sun rising over the rugged snow-capped mountain peaks was absolutely stunning.

"It's like watching a painting," Jack said.

"I never thought of it that way," I said, enjoying the relative warmth of the sun on my face.

"I rarely miss a sunrise," he said.

"But you said you're from Houston." I knew from experience that watching the sunrise in the city could be challenging. The views just weren't all that good.

"I'm lucky I have a good view," he said, before abruptly changing the subject. "I haven't had a home-cooked breakfast like this in forever."

"I'm surprised my mother hasn't already cooked breakfast

for you. It's sort of her thing."

"She's offered on more than one occasion," he said. "But I didn't want her to go to any trouble."

"She likes to make breakfast on Christmas Eve morning," I said, remembering. It was something I had all but forgotten.

Most people probably made breakfast on Christmas Day morning, but our family did most of our celebrations on Christmas Eve day.

It explained why I had a preference for Christmas Eve over Christmas Day.

By the time Christmas Day arrived, everything was starting to go back to normal and though I didn't go around telling people, I started to feel a little sad that it was all over.

I bit into a bite of bacon and swept my windblown hair out of my eyes.

I caught Jack gazing at me, his expression full of curiosity.

"What?" I asked.

"I know you don't live in Whiskey Springs," he said. "But I don't know where you live."

Jack had lived with my parents for long enough that one of them should have mentioned that their daughter—their only daughter—lives in Pittsburgh.

"They didn't tell you," I said, fighting to keep the moisture out of my eyes. Either that or maybe Jack had forgotten, something I doubted very much.

His answer told me so much about him. His answer told me that he was a good man.

"I'm sure they did," he said. "I probably just forgot."

He didn't seem like the kind of person to forget much of anything.

I just looked at him, knowing he was being kind.

I didn't fault my parents. They had adapted to my brother and me not being here.

My teeth chattered, just a little, and I shivered.

"It's cold," he said. "We should go in and get warmed up."

"Sounds good," I said.

Before I could move to gather up our plates and cups back onto the wooden tray we'd brought outside to the little table, Jack had everything stacked up nicely.

"If you'll get the door," he said. "I'll get this."

I opened the door and stepped inside, the warmth spilling over me, making me shiver anew.

We walked in companionable silence to the kitchen.

Daddy was standing there, staring at the cappuccino machine with a perplexed expression.

"Good morning," he said, looking at us over his shoulder.

"Good morning," we said.

Daddy scratched his chin and looked over at Jack. Watched him start unpacking the tray.

"Something happened to the coffee machine," Daddy said.

I didn't miss the way Jack hid a smile.

But even more importantly, I didn't miss the look that passed between the two of us.

And I found myself smiling.

"We'll grab coffee at the coffee shop," Daddy said to Jack. "We need to make a house call."

So much for impressing my father with either the coffee machine or my breakfast skills.

As they bundled up and left through the door leading to the garage, I sat down at the kitchen table.

Nothing about this trip was going as planned.

I needed to stop thinking about Jack.

About the way his blue eyes shimmered in the early morning sunlight.

About the way he smiled as he looked at me.

I shook my head and finished cleaning up.

My mother would be down soon and I could make her

coffee with their new machine. Maybe even whip her up some fresh eggs.

Maybe coming in and making breakfast for my parents hadn't been the best idea as far as they were concerned.

But it worked out well with Jack.

Having breakfast with Jack on the second-floor balcony had been an unexpected surprise.

One I needed to stop thinking about now. It was better if I didn't think about Jack at all.

But then just as I had managed to put him out of my thoughts for a full two minutes, I saw his charcoal gray wool scarf draped across the back of one of the kitchen chairs.

I picked it up, thinking to take it to him, but then I heard the sound of the garage lumbering down.

I draped the scarf around my neck and took a moment to breath in his scent. An earthy leathery scent mixed with the old-fashioned clean scent of soap.

Scolding myself, I took the scarf and hung it on a hangar in the coat closet next to my wool coat.

I resolutely closed the door. I was thinking about him far too much.

I needed something to distract myself with.

14

JACK

*D*oc Alexander had two vehicles. He had a newer SUV, one that I enjoyed riding in.

I hadn't brought a car to Whiskey Springs. Doc had assured me that I would not need a car. That he had a car I could use if I needed transportation.

Since I'd come from Houston, a driving city, it had been weird at first, but it had turned out that I actually had not needed a vehicle. At least not yet.

Unfortunately, the vehicle that Doc let me drive was the same vehicle we were riding in now.

An old 1965 green Ford truck. For a truck that was nearly sixty years old, it ran smooth as silk.

Doc kept it up himself, tinkering with it in his garage when he wasn't medically treating someone around town.

We headed west, deeper into the mountains away from town, traveling up in elevation.

"Where are we headed?" I asked, but I knew perfectly well where. We were headed to the Daniels House.

"One of the staff members is expecting a baby," he said, shifting gears.

"Grace," I said with a little nod.

"Good memory," Doc said. "I didn't see any point in her driving to town when we could go to her."

"I'm sure she appreciates that," I said, although I really didn't know. I had yet to figure out the intricacies of small town life. Sometimes people wanted to get out for a drive and other times they wanted to avoid it.

Wasn't sure I would ever figure it out. I think a person had to be born and bred here to really have a good sense of how things worked.

I'd have to ask Bella. Since she had lived somewhere else, she might be able to shed some light on how things worked here as opposed to the city.

Doc had never lived anywhere else, so he only had one perspective.

What I did know about Grace, that Doc didn't seem to think I knew, was that Grace was like me in that she had no vehicle.

I had read her chart during one of my many downtimes. I'd found her interesting because she was like me in so many ways. Including not being from here and not having her own vehicle. I also found it interesting that Doc found it noteworthy to include that particular fact in his chart.

Probably there to remind him that she would need a house call when he saw her.

Doc could have driven up here himself and probably would have unless he had a reason.

Maybe there was something unusual about Grace's pregnancy.

Turns out I was on the wrong path with that one. This trip wasn't about Grace at all.

"You've met my daughter," he said.

"Yes sir." His statement made me feel like I'd done

something wrong. Had I? Was I not allowed to have breakfast with the boss's daughter?

"What are your thoughts?" he asked, catching me off guard.

"She's nice," I said, then added. "And very lovely." He wanted to know what I thought. He'd know that I noticed how beautiful she was and if I said nothing, he'd know that I had given it entirely too much thought and was trying to keep it from him.

He kept his eyes on the road and nodded. "Always had trouble with that one and the boys."

"Is that so?" I asked. This was turning out to be a most interesting conversation. More interesting, I had to admit, than the expectant mother we were going to visit.

"When she was in high school, that girl dated every boy in Whiskey Springs," he said. "Brought them all home, too."

I cleared my throat. I didn't know Bella very well, but I had a feeling she wouldn't like me knowing this. She struck me as a private person.

And hearing about her high school adventures seemed a bit like an invasion of privacy.

"She sounds like my sister," I said. My sister wouldn't appreciate me talking about her either, but I needed to normalize what Doc was saying about his daughter.

I didn't know what purpose he could have for telling me this. I could think that maybe he was trying to warn me away from her.

He didn't need to worry. I knew better than to get too close to her, but only because she lived in Pittsburg.

And then there was the fact that her father was my boss, even if it was only for a year. It was a year that barely gotten off the ground.

Doc shifted gears and turned a curve that led into an especially steep incline. Looking out the window, I saw nothing but a steep—very steep and rocky—drop off.

I shifted in my seat and sat up straighter. The mountains were beautiful and all that to look at from a distance, but being this close up and personal, only inches away from certain death, I could do without.

"I got tired of meeting all the young high school boys her age."

I bit back a laugh. Sounded rather normal to me and said a lot that she brought the boys home instead of just going out with them.

I was trying to figure out a nice way to ask him why he was telling me this when he announced that the Daniels House was just up ahead.

Either this conversation would have to wait, or even more preferable, perhaps we had finished it.

I wanted to know all about Bella, but I didn't want to hear the things from her past that bothered her father.

I wanted to know about her now. Maybe this had something to do with the reason she rarely came home.

If he was trying to frighten me away, he was achieving the very opposite.

I was even more intrigued with Bella Alexander.

15

BELLA

*A*fter I cleaned up the kitchen, I packed all the food—the cooked bacon, eggs, and biscuits—away in the refrigerator. Apparently, my time could have been better spent doing something besides cooking.

I pulled on my woolen coat, my gloves, and my hat and headed out the front door.

I decided that a latte from the coffee shop was as good an excuse to get out and take a walk as any.

Stepping outside in the wind, I remembered to wrap my scarf around my face. Still... the sting of the wind burned my eyes.

A white Christmas was not in the forecast, but it was going to snow.

I could feel it. As the old people would say, I could feel it in my bones.

I would bet money that we were going to have a white Christmas here in Whiskey Springs.

I passed the house where Tommy Burns had lived. The tree house where we had plotted our futures was gone now and the yard was neat and tidily groomed by someone who did not appear to have children.

Tommy was one of two serious boyfriends I'd had in high school. I'd gone out with three other boys, but they hadn't been interesting. Those three wanted to stay in Whiskey Springs, so I quickly lost interest. We did not understand each other.

Tommy, at least, wanted to be an astronaut and I wanted to go to college. Get a degree in finance.

I didn't know what Tommy was doing now, but I knew he was most certainly not an astronaut. Last I heard, he was working down at the lumberyard.

Somewhere during the first semester of my sophomore year I had dropped the business classes and made a smooth transition over to psychology.

There was nothing wrong with business. It had just seemed so... serious.

I didn't have a crystal ball, but if I had stayed in finance, I saw myself in a job without any kind of joy.

In the meantime, I had taken to my first two basic psychology classes like a duck to water.

I blamed my father. He was always talking to me about his theories about why people did the things they did.

He had instilled in me a curiosity about human nature before I could even walk good.

So I hadn't even told my parents until the next year. I had kept my change of heart to myself.

I didn't want anyone talking me out of it and the way I'd figured it, not telling anyone was the best way to avoid that.

To be so curious about other people, I preferred to keep my personal business to myself.

Could be why I never really felt like I belonged in the small town.

I felt the city suited me much more.

But right now, hardly anyone in Whiskey Springs knew who I was. A few people would recognize me, of course.

I stepped into the coffee shop to the scent of rich, aromatic coffee. There was nothing like the scent of expresso. Even at home, somehow coffee just never smelled so rich and strong as it did in a coffee shop.

There were a dozen people inside, even this early in the day.

There were five people ahead of me in line. And the young girl, probably a college student behind the counter didn't appear to be in any hurry.

She was, in fact, quite friendly with everyone.

I wasn't worried about the wait. I used the time to just relax and look around. To see how, if any, things had changed since I had been here last time.

The coffee machines had been updated, of course. That was one thing about Mr. Gray, the owner. He kept things modern. He understood that you had to put money back into the business to keep it up.

One of things from my finance major days that had stuck with me. If I ever struck out on my own, which I just might do one day, I would remember that.

The Christmas song playing on the radio was nostalgic and reminded me of my teenage years, before I had any real responsibilities. When my job was just to study and fight my parents for my independence.

My father had always been a little funny about me. He didn't want me to date until I was sixteen. And then he still didn't like it. It was my mother who had fought for me. Who had gotten Daddy to agree to let me date at fifteen. Fifteen was still much later than my peers began to date.

I knew why. I knew exactly why. It had everything to do with my aunt—Daddy's sister.

"Good morning," the girl behind the counter said with a large grin when it was my turn to order. "How can I help you?"

I ordered a latte, soy milk, extra vanilla, with caramel drizzle. I knew the caramel drizzle added sugar that I was trying to avoid, but I was feeling a bit self-indulgent at the moment.

I waited the few minutes it took for them to make my coffee, then I took the green paper cup wrapped in a cardboard sleeve and sat at one of the empty tables next to the window.

The clouds were gathering again around the rugged mountain peaks. A sure sign that it was going to snow. I was thinking it would hold off until tonight though.

Tonight my mother would drag me to the Festival of Trees.

She would have some kind of decorating theme like birds or candy. All the participants did. Then people would come in and vote. The winner just got a little token, nothing big, but they would get their names and picture in the local paper.

It was quite an honor to win the Festival of Trees decorating contest.

My thoughts made their way back to Jack. I'd actually kept them at bay longer than I had expected.

I wondered if he would be going to the festival or if he would stay at home.

Somebody, either Jack or my father, I mused, would need to be at the festival in case anyone had a medical emergency. Maybe even both of them would be there.

At any rate, seeing my father nudge him away from me this morning brought back memories of my teenage days.

I'd brought a few boys home. My mother thought that if my father met the boys I went out with he would be more comfortable with me dating them.

I never really thought it helped very much.

And some things, it seemed, never changed.

Not that I was dating Jack.

Or even thinking about dating Jack.

Not in the least.

JACK

*T*he Daniels House was big enough to hold half a dozen families.

The story was that it had been built in the late 1800s by a man who somehow mysteriously fell into a ton of money. He had quietly been one of the richest men in the country.

The Daniels House had been one of the most modern in the west. They had the money for indoor plumbing before anyone else in the town of Whiskey Springs. And the oddest thing was they lived far out of town. And still did. And still the Daniels House was meticulously maintained.

Sometimes they rented rooms to people looking for a bed and breakfast, not because they needed the money, but because they enjoyed meeting new people.

The Daniels were the first ones to get snowed in during a storm.

I learned all this from Doc as we waited for Grace to finish up in the kitchen before making her way to the study for her appointment.

"I think you need to focus on light work," he told Grace

after a quick exam. "And you'll need to come in the office for an ultrasound next time."

"I can't," Grace said, so softly we could barely hear her words.

"Why not?" Doc asked.

"I don't have a way to get there." Grace lowered her head, looking at the floor.

"What about the father? Does he have a vehicle?" Doc persisted.

Grace shook her head.

"A car? A truck?"

"I don't know how to find the father," Grace whispered.

I saw the rage in Doc's expression.

I didn't understand it, but I saw it.

This might be a small town, but surely he saw unwed mothers from time to time. Even mothers like Grace who were on their own.

"We'll come and get you," Doc said. "When it's time for you to come in to town for your exam."

Grace nodded. Swallowed hard. "Can I go now?"

"Of course," Doc said.

Grace wasted no time darting from the room. We heard a door close soundly in the direction of the staff rooms off from the kitchen.

Doc stared straight ahead. Not saying anything. Not moving. I'd never seen Doc so quiet.

"Are you alright?" I asked, needing to know, but dreading his answer. He looked like he was ready to explode.

Doc took a breath as though he suddenly remembered to breathe.

"It's such a waste."

I kept my mouth closed out of respect for Doc's age. Single women had babies all the time and they made good mothers.

But Doc was from an old world where a woman was looked down upon if she had a baby without a husband.

I was surprised that he was having this kind of reaction. It seemed so different from the man I'd come to know.

Then I knew that it was something else entirely. Not judgement. It was pain.

"I can't save her," he said, rubbing his chin. "I couldn't save my sister either."

*M*y mother had chosen a red forest theme for the tree competition.

The two of us stood looking at the undecorated blue spruce standing in front of us.

Our tree was one of twelve. The trees all looked pretty much alike right now. But in a couple of hours, that would change. In a couple of hours, they would all look distinctively different.

For the moment, at least, voices were hushed in the high school gym where the bleachers had been pushed back against the walls. There was music though, in the background. Old music. Sounded like Frank Sinatra. One of the classics.

Two banker's boxes at our feet.

I opened the one closest to me and rummaged carefully through the foam birds with bright red feathers and a clip at the bottom of each one to attach them to the tree branches.

"These are handmade?" I asked. They were all red birds with dark beaks and dark rimmed eyes. Cardinals.

They were almost alike, but there were minute differences that suggested they were not made by a machine.

Momma took the lid off the other box, revealing similar sized white cardinals. The solid white cardinals had black eyes and long fluffy tails.

"They are handmade," she said with a glance of appreciation in my direction. "Or so they say."

"I believe it." I held up two of the red birds and compared them. The stitches were a little wider on one than the other, but the overall pattern was the same. On further scrutiny, I noticed that the shades of red were darker on one than the other, but that wasn't unusual.

This was one of the many projects Momma worked on throughout the year. First deciding on her theme, then searching out the perfect decorations.

Being part of the Whiskey Springs community, especially being the physician's wife brought with it certain expectation of participation. But I'd never once heard her complain.

I glanced around the room at some of the other participants opening up their boxes. I recognized some of them. Mr. Gray from the coffee shop and a couple of his girls. The preacher's wife with a team around her. There was going to be some fierce competition this year.

"We're just doing red and white cardinals?" I asked.

Surely Momma wasn't just using birds as her theme.

Then I caught sight of Jack coming in through the door, carrying two cardboard boxes. If Momma answered me, I didn't hear her.

Without so much as a hitch in his stride, he spotted us and headed over.

He smiled at me when he reached my side setting a flutter of butterflies loose in my stomach.

This was the first time I had seen him today after my father had dragged him away.

"There are three more boxes in the truck," he said.

"I'll help you," I said quickly, surprising myself. But I wanted to go with him. I wanted to be alone with Jack even if it was for just a few minutes.

I didn't question it. I just went with it. I'd think about it later.

We got plenty of curious looks as the two of us walked through the gym to the door.

Everyone would know who Jack was by now. Only a few of the more astute people would recognize me. Not only had I been gone long enough that the children were adults now, but I liked to think that I looked different. More sophisticated.

I was no longer the cheerleader with the long straight hair. I was a college professor with long wavy hair.

Jack pushed the door open and I stepped outside into the brisk cold air. It was more windy than it had been less than an hour ago.

"It's going to snow tonight," I said.

"It's already snowing up at the Daniels House," he said, opening the passenger door to the old 1965 green Ford truck.

"Daddy let you drive his truck?" I asked, biting my lip.

"It's the vehicle he assigned me," he said. "I guess it's better than nothing."

So Jack had come to Whiskey Springs without a truck.

I was really starting to feel bad for him.

"This one is light," he said, handing me a square cardboard box about twelve inches by twelve inches.

I took the box from him. He was right. It was so light I wasn't sure there was anything in it.

"What's in here?" I asked.

"I don't know. I just do what your mother tells me."

I bit back a laugh as he grabbed the other two boxes and closed the door with his shoulder.

My mother hadn't said anything to me about Jack, but if he was doing what she wanted, he was in trouble.

No telling what she'd have him doing. Momma was not one to let good help pass her by.

We carried the boxes back inside to our tree and looked around.

"Where's your mother?" Jack asked.

"I don't know."

A middle-aged lady with a clipboard came to stand next to us. She wore black rimmed glasses and a name tag identifying herself as Mrs. Mary Crane. She had a stern look about her. She reminded me of my third grade math teacher who threatened to rap our knuckles if we didn't learn our multiplication tables.

"Mrs. Alexander had to leave," she said, her lips pursed, looking from me to Jack and back again.

"Why?" I asked. "Is everything okay?"

"She just said she had to help Doc with something. I'm supposed to tell you not to worry."

I pulled my cell out of my back pocket. When did Momma forget how to text? Surely she still knew how to make a phone call if nothing else.

"Thank you," I said, as Mrs. Crane walked off, obviously having more important things to do than converse with us.

Jack and I exchanged a look.

"What are we supposed to do?" Jack asked when Mrs. Crane was out of earshot.

I shrugged. "Decorate the tree," I said, then looked at him, my brows furrowed. "Do you know how to decorate a tree?"

"How hard can it be?" he asked.

I smiled to myself and began taking the lids off all the boxes.

No matter how much prep Momma had put into this year's tree, I was pretty sure that we weren't going to win this year.

Jack, kneeling on the floor, looked up at me. "There are a lot of birds here," he said.

"That's the theme," I said, but my gaze locked onto his and I realized I wasn't going to be much more help than he was.

When he smiled at me, I could barely keep my thoughts from tangling into a knot.

Looking back down at the red birds, I sighed. There were worse places to be.

18

JACK

*T*he high school gym was packed even though the doors to the public weren't supposed to open until five o'clock. The public, it seemed, had not gotten the memo.

People were already walking around, children running, while we tried to figure out just how we were going to make our tree presentable.

With about fifty cardinals for decoration—some red and some white.

I'd never seen so many bird decorations in one place. They reminded me of the black grackles that tended to congregate in Houston parking lots. They would swarm in and cover both the cars and the asphalt in black. Always a creepy sight, in my opinion, although some people thought the grackle should be named the official bird of Houston.

"What are you thinking?" Bella asked, sitting back on her heels, looking at me.

"What do you mean?" I put my hands on my hips, wondering why we couldn't just be like normal people and use balls to decorate the tree.

She smiled. "You've got a funny look on your face."

Her smile dispelled any concern I had about what to do about the birds. We'd figure something out.

"I was just thinking about the black birds in the Houston parking lots."

"The what?"

"Never mind," I said and pulled the lid off one of the other boxes. At least it didn't have birds. Just bird nests.

Well hell. The birds had to have someplace to nest.

"You don't like birds," she said, with a little knowing smile.

"I don't dislike them," I said. "There are just so many of them."

"I agree," she said. "But I think we just need to trust the process." I wasn't quite sure what she meant by that, but I trusted her.

"You're the boss," I said.

"How did I get to be the boss?"

I pulled all the bird nests out and lined them up. "You're the boss's daughter and she's not here, so it's by default."

She didn't say anything for a minute. Then she just shrugged.

"I guess if I can navigate hundreds of students through a semester, I can get us through the decoration of a Christmas tree."

"You're a teacher?" I realized I really did not know anything about this woman I was crushing on.

"A college professor," she said, keeping her expression blank.

And again, I wondered why her parents hadn't told me that. Most parents wanted to brag on their children. But not the Alexanders.

They mentioned Bella and Charlie now and then, sure, but both of them had left out any details.

I found it quite rather unusual.

"I'm surprised my parents didn't tell you that."

"They're surprisingly private about you and your brother."

"At least you know I have a brother," she said, with a little shake of her head. "I guess they're mad at us for going off to live somewhere else."

"Maybe," I said, knowing it wasn't what she wanted to hear. But I had a little bit more insight now than I had before my trip with Doc up to the Daniels House this morning.

"You're no help," she said, lining up the white birds much like I had the bird nests.

"Your father told me about his sister."

"Oh." She sat back and looked at me, the scowl back on her face. "That's different."

"Yeah," I said. "I don't think he really meant to tell me. It just sort of came up."

"Well." She began unboxing the red birds. I liked the white ones with the long tails better, but there were more red ones. "He never talks about her."

"I'm sorry," I said.

"Don't apologize. It all happened before I was even born."

I nodded. "I rather figured that out. But still…" It probably wasn't my place to bring this up. In fact, I'd have to say that it most definitely was not my place. Unfortunately I felt compelled to do it anyway. "I think maybe it's affected how he's treated you."

She looked startled for a second, but quickly masked it by dragging the lightweight square box to her and opening it.

She pulled out a big white owl that was obviously the tree topper. She held it out for me to see. "Guess we know what's in the box now," she said.

"We usually have a star on the top of our tree."

She put the owl back in the box. "We have an angel at home, but this tree isn't for us."

Bella didn't seem to want to talk about her family, so I left it alone.

I suppose in all fairness she didn't know me well enough. I already knew I shouldn't have brought up something so personal.

Maybe she'd talk to me about it later.

Right now we had a tree to decorate. Seeing the one next to us decorated with fishing poles and... fish... brought out my competitive spirit.

I was going to tuck my wariness of birds aside and see if we couldn't make this the best-looking tree in the gym.

Surely working with the best-looking girl in the room wouldn't hurt.

19

BELLA

*T*wo hours later, I stood back and scrutinized our newly decorated Christmas tree.

I liked the bright red and clean white decorations. Everything was either red or white except for the birds' nests that we'd tucked in among the needles. The brown straw nests blended into the tree quite nicely.

Jack had been right though. He was right about a lot of things, but he was most certainly right about there being a lot of birds.

The tree looked like it might take flight at any moment.

"It looks good," Jack said, standing next to me, also examining our work.

"You're just being kind," I said, not even looking at him.

"I like the colors."

I bit my lip. A diplomatic answer if I'd ever heard one.

He turned in a circle, scanning the room. Then stopped, facing me, and looked into my eyes.

"I think we stand a chance of winning," he said, leaning close so no one else would hear, as though saying it would somehow decrease our chances.

"Now I know you're delusional."

"Come on," he said with a discreet nod over his shoulder. "Fish?"

I bit back a laugh. It wasn't nice to laugh at other people's work. I had to admit, though, I'd never seen a Christmas tree decorated with fish. Similar to our bird ornaments, it was covered in fish ornaments, mostly blue and green. They had little tackle boxes and even fish on a stringer.

"Birds," I said.

He laughed.

I loved his laugh.

I loved the way his whole face lit up when he smiled. It made his eyes look deep as indigo. Then the light would change and they would shift to a deep ocean blue.

I was fascinated by the way the light changed the color of his eyes.

"You gotta admit the ombre one is nice," I said, admiring the one to our left decorated in a gradient fashion. It was decorated with simple colored glass balls, but the bottom third was in fuchsia, then a row of mulberry purple. The middle third was in cobalt blue, followed by a row of shamrock green balls, and the top third was canary yellow.

He winced. "Yeah. I think they might be our biggest competition."

"I'd vote for them," I said.

"Can we vote?"

"That would be illegal," I said, with a nod toward the preacher's wife and her team. If they voted for themselves, it would definitely tip the scales in their favor.

"I guess it wouldn't be fair." He stuck his hands in his pockets. "So what do we do now? Just stand here next to our tree?"

"And look silly," I added for him, with a sideways smile. "I think we can take a break. Do you like hot chocolate?"

"Who doesn't?"

I thought of my ex-boyfriend who only drank white chocolate which wasn't even really chocolate. "Good point," I said. "There's a shop down the street with THE best hot chocolate."

He grinned. "Let's go."

After we bundled up, we walked through the crowded gym, mostly being ignored this time.

Stepping outside, the cold air was like a slap in the face, reminding me again to wrap my scarf around my mouth and nose.

Christmas music spilled from speakers along the sidewalk and everything twinkled or glittered. With the light flakes falling, it was a winter wonderland.

I turned to the right. Hopefully Smedley's Ice Cream Shop was still there. I hadn't checked. I had just assumed it would be.

Three doors down, we stood in front of their doors. It was still there.

"We're here," I said.

"We're getting hot chocolate at an ice cream shop?" he asked, looking clearly skeptical.

"Just trust me," I said, crossing my fingers that they still had the hot chocolate with ice cream balls. I'd never seen it on a menu anywhere else.

"I trust you," he said, just before he opened the door and held it for me to walk through.

A simple statement. One uttered millions of times every day. But something about Jack saying those words to me sent little shivers up and down my spine.

He was trouble.

The kind of trouble a girl couldn't resist. This girl, anyway.

20

JACK

*B*eing in the ice cream shop—Smedley's Ice Cream Shop—was like stepping back into a different time. The 1950s maybe.

There were a dozen little round wooden tables with matching wooden chairs. Half the tables and chairs were red and half were white.

Seemed to be the color combination of the day.

The chairs were almost too small for a grown man to sit in, which I found interesting since those sitting at the three tables other than ours were all adults.

A pop Christmas song streamed through the speakers, blending seamlessly with customer's voices.

Bella had been right.

This was the best host chocolate I had ever tasted.

It was hot chocolate with little balls of what might be ice cream floating inside. Whatever it was, it was soft and sweet and the mix of the cold and the hot chocolate was compelling.

"Do you like it?" Bella asked with a grin. She was eating the ice cream out of her hot chocolate with a spoon.

I was sipping mine with a straw. Apparently, it was a flexible concoction. "I do like it. And I've never had anything like it."

"It's the only place I've ever seen it."

"And you're from Houston," she said with a lift of her brows. "Bigger than Pittsburgh."

"A little," I said, giving up on the straw and using my spoon. It was burning my tongue anyway.

"Have you ever been to Pittsburgh?" she asked.

"I don't think so," I said. I had flown to a lot of places with my grandfather and countless other relatives who were pilots, but if I'd been to Pittsburgh, it had not been memorable.

"It's nice," she said. "They've done a lot with downtown over the past decade or so. A lot of cultural things. Museums. Restaurants. Theatres."

"Sounds nice. You live downtown." I was making an assumption.

"No," she said with a little smile and another bite of ice cream. "I ride the subway."

This girl lived in Pittsburgh and obviously knew her way around the city.

Why was it that the thought of her riding the subway by herself made me worry for her.

It wasn't my place to say anything though and my sudden burst of concern was surprising.

"It's safe," she said with a little smile.

"Good to know."

"What about you? Have you always lived in Houston?"

"Born and bred," I said. It was a vague and, granted, a true answer, but it left out some pertinent details. No need to tell her right now that I spent a few years in Boston when I was in medical school at Harvard.

Things were so relaxed right now between us. I didn't want

to risk it. Sometimes people were intimidated when they found out that I had gone to Harvard.

Of course, Bella was a college professor, so I doubted it would bother her so much.

I was still trying to figure this out when we were interrupted.

"Bella Alexander?"

Bella blinked and looked up at a man standing at our table. He was about my age. Not bad looking. A little rough around the edges.

"Tommy?" Bella said, setting her spoon down.

"I thought it was you," Tommy said, grinning like a loon. "You don't look one bit different."

"I guess I'll take that as a compliment," Bella said, but I could tell that she didn't. "This is my friend Jack. Jack this is an old friend from high school. Tommy."

"Nice to meet you, Tommy," I said.

"Likewise," Tommy glanced briefly—barely—in my direction, but his interest was obviously on Bella. "Are you back?"

"No," she said, obviously knowing that he meant back living here. "I'm visiting for the holidays."

Tommy nodded. "It's been a while."

"A little while." She nodded in agreement.

"What are you doing now?" he asked.

"I'm a college professor," she said with a glance at me.

How could he not know that? Bella had left here, gone out in the world and become successful and no one here even knew it.

I bit my tongue. I wanted to tell everyone how successful she was.

But it wasn't my place.

Not my place at all.

It was just my place to admire her.

Maybe it was better that everyone didn't know.

I wasn't sure it would serve my interests if all the guys here in Whiskey Springs admired her half as much as I did.

21

BELLA

I sat back in my red wooden chair and watched Tommy walk up to the counter and place an order.

It was noisy now. A group of four college students had come inside and were taking their time ordering. Laughing and chatting in that easy-going college student way.

It was funny. I felt nothing for Tommy other than a vague curiosity.

Maybe it was to be expected. I rarely ever even thought about him. When I left Whiskey Springs, I'd been so excited about the possibilities in the world before me that I didn't even really miss him back then.

I turned my gaze back to Jack and shrugged. He was watching me with those fathomless blue eyes. Eyes that weren't smiling so much right now.

"And I thought I'd changed over the past… decade," I said.

"He's an idiot," Jack said without hesitation. Then seemed to think better. "Everybody changes."

"You're right," I said. "If people didn't change, I doubt psychology would be a profession."

He looked at me, his head tilted to one side as though he was considering. "I think you might be right."

"I'm right," I said, picking up my spoon and taking a sip of hot chocolate that had cooled off and didn't taste so good now.

"Is Tommy an old boyfriend?" he asked.

"Why do you ask that?" For some reason I didn't really want Jack to know that I'd dated Tommy. Even if it was in high school. Forever ago.

"Because he keeps looking over here."

I felt my face heat.

Glancing over at Tommy, I saw that Jack was right. Tommy saw me looking at him and grinned. With a shake of my head, I looked away quickly.

"We hung out in high school," I said, taking a deep breath. "I guess you'd call him an old boyfriend. We went to the prom together and all that. But..." I stopped, realizing I was telling Jack more than I had intended.

"But he wanted to stay here and you wanted to move away," he said.

I glanced dubiously at Jack. Maybe my parents had talked to him about me after all.

"It's just kinda obvious," he said. "In a good romance, you two would end up back together."

I shuddered. "No. Please don't wish that on me."

"He seems like a nice guy," Jack said, but I knew he was teasing me.

"He is. He's a perfectly nice guy. But we're too different. Besides I think he has a wife and about a dozen or so kids."

"A dozen?" Jack asked.

"Well, maybe not quite that many, but a lot."

Jack nodded. "And children aren't on your ten-year plan." He sat back, pushing his glass aside next to mine.

I couldn't tell what he was trying to say. He was looking away now, his brow creased.

"They're not not on my agenda. I've just been rather busy." I forced myself not to sound defensive.

"Yeah," he said, running a hand through his hair and glancing back at me. "I get it. Same here."

"No family yet?" I asked, looking at him with interest now. Glad to have the conversation focused away from myself.

"No rush," he said, watching people, bundled up to the hilt, hurrying along the sidewalk.

There were more than just a few flurries of snow now. The snow was falling more like a light mist.

"I have plenty of nieces and nephews," he said.

I would never know what possessed me in the next moment. It was something I didn't talk about. It wasn't like I wanted him to do anything about it. It just seemed like something I should tell him in this moment.

"My brother and I are the end of the family line."

"I know," he said. "Your brother is engaged, though, right?"

"Right..." I said with a strong level of suspicion. "Didn't know you knew that."

"You hang around a family a little while and you pick up a few things."

I could only imagine. It was odd. Coming home to spend time with my family and finding Jack. My family who didn't talk much about me.

And Jack who seemed to want to know everything.

22

JACK

*A*s we walked in silence back to the gym and the Festive of Trees, bundled up in our coats and scarves, the snow began falling in earnest.

I'd seen my share of snow in Boston, but the snow here seemed different. Probably a result of the higher elevation and the tall, rugged mountains that surrounded us on just about every side.

In Boston, the people got friendlier when it snowed. I hadn't been here long enough to find out whether that was true in Whiskey Springs or not. Since Christmas was an intervening variable, I didn't have enough information to know the answer yet. About the snow.

At any rate, as I walked along the crowded sidewalk next to Bella, I realized that I was relieved that she was single. She hadn't come right out and said so, but I could tell that she was. I had enough cousins to know when someone was single.

I was still thinking about going into psychiatry. It wasn't too late. My Grandmother Savannah, a renowned psychologist, had suggested that route to me on more than one occasion.

She'd noticed that I was a natural observer of human behavior. And, it seemed, I was rather good at it.

But that was for later. I could look into some applications, but right now, I needed to get through this residence. And at this particular moment, I was more interested in focusing on Bella than work.

I'd asked Bella about her ten-year plan. I didn't have one. Everyone told me I needed one. But I knew what direction I wanted to go.

Medicine. As for specifics, I didn't know yet. I felt like I needed more information before I decided.

It was a decision I didn't think I needed to rush into. So I eschewed the ten-year plan at the risk of seeming a bit negligent to all my cohorts.

They could have their ten-year plan if they wanted to. I, on the other hand, wanted to keep my options open.

My grandmother—the same grandmother who suggested psychiatry for me—taught me from a young age to keep my options open in life.

Don't be rigid. Always be open to possibilities.

I knew that she wasn't being literal about everything, but her words had sunk in enough to make me wary of ruling things out.

It was an interesting combination. I followed rules, but I kept the rules for my own life open.

If I hadn't, I wouldn't have ended up here. And. I wouldn't have met Bella.

I wasn't sure what the implications of that were yet, but I knew there was something.

I just had to figure it out.

We stepped back inside the warmth of the gym, now even more crowded than it had been before we'd taken our walk down the street.

Mrs. Alexander was waiting at our tree for us.

"I'm impressed with the decorating job you two did on the tree."

Bella looked at me and grinned. "Dr. Jack Fleming and I make a good team. Don't we?"

I grinned back. I couldn't help it. Bella Alexander was irresistible.

"I think we stand a good chance of winning," I said.

Bella and her mother exchanged one of those mother-daughter looks.

Mrs. Alexander leaned over and said in a stage whisper. "He's a gentleman."

Bella nodded and bit her lip.

I didn't know what one had to do with the other. If anything.

All I knew at this particular moment was that Pittsburgh much too far away from both Whiskey Springs and Houston.

23

BELLA

*T*he gym was loud. It couldn't have been much louder if there had been a basketball game going on.

Between the children running and squealing and the music that someone seemed keep turning up. It was almost like the two—the people and the music—were in a competition, each getting louder and louder.

But it was a festive, happy loud, so I didn't mind.

We didn't win. But we did get an honorable mention which was essentially fourth place.

The ombre tree that I liked came in second. Disappointing. And the one with the fish decorations came in third. Ahead of us. Incomprehensible.

Maybe the public had a sense of humor.

The one that came in first place looked like an ordinary tree to me. Glass balls. An angel on top. Red ribbons wrapped around and tucked prettily in between the limbs.

People, it seemed, had an odd mixture of traditional and downright weird.

I could see that Jack was disappointed.

He stood a few minutes and studied the tree with the fish decorations.

"I have an idea for next year," he said, seriously.

I looked at Jack sideways.

Next year.

I knew for a fact that medical residences only lasted for one year. That meant that Jack was either just talking to be talking or he was thinking something he wasn't telling.

Whichever way it was, I found it a little vexing.

I looked at him sideways, not trying to hide my annoyance. He just grinned. And that annoyed me even more.

I was about to remind him that he wouldn't be here next year, but then I decided it didn't matter.

"I'll be back," I said, turning without explanation and walking toward the ladies room.

I just needed to take a minute for myself. To get my thoughts back in order.

Christmas was a magical time of year. A time when possibilities were endless and everything was sparkling.

I sat at a little vanity chair in front of the ladies room mirror and swept a touch of red lipstick across my lips.

Maybe Jack had simply gotten carried away in the moment.

I smiled to myself. It was sweet really. A lesser man would have made it a point to tell us that we were on our own next year.

I liked Jack. My mother was right. He was a gentleman.

When I was a girl, about age thirteen, I had told my mother that I was going to grow up and marry a gentleman.

She had laughed at the time, but it had stuck.

Whenever I dated someone new, she would ask me if he was a gentleman.

That became our code that told her whether I thought the guy was a keeper.

This was the first time Momma had volunteered to decide

for me, but it was true that she knew Jack better than I did at this point.

So my mother thought Jack was a keeper.

Interesting.

And a little disconcerting. Because I kinda felt that way, too.

Stepping back out into the gym, I looked toward our tree for Jack. But he wasn't there. I quickly scanned the room. I didn't see him.

I stood frozen right there in the middle of the floor.

My mother was standing at our tree talking to Mrs. Crane, still holding her clipboard.

Jack was nowhere to be seen.

I made a turn, looking for him. Maybe he had been called out for an emergency.

Rubbing my hands on my jeans, I kept walking.

Then I saw him.

He was standing with a pretty young lady. The young lady had a perky blonde ponytail and she was looking at Jack like she wanted to jump his bones.

Jack was turned sideways, so I couldn't really see his expression, but he was nodding at something the girl was saying.

I didn't recognize her. She was younger than me. Probably a college student.

The spurt of jealousy surprised and alarmed me.

But this was how it was supposed to be.

I lived in Pittsburgh. Had a life in Pittsburgh.

Jack lived in Whiskey Springs. He would be here for a full year and maybe even longer.

It was possible that he would decide to stay here. To make a life for himself here. It was even more likely if he met a girl here that he liked.

I walked blindly toward our tree.

Reaching the tree, I just stood there, staring at one of the white birds with the long feathers.

I knew better than to get too close. I just knew better.

I took a deep breath and steeled myself. Only a few more days and I would be back to my normal life.

I could put all thoughts of Jack behind me.

24

JACK

I watched Bella across the crowded room as she came back from the ladies room.

The gym had gotten uncomfortably crowded. It was mostly the children running around squealing that increased the volume in the room.

It didn't mind the children. I had enough nieces and nephews that they didn't bother me at all.

It didn't help that the music—good music as far as I could tell which wasn't very far—seemed to keep getting louder and louder.

Right now, whatever song was playing... I couldn't even tell what it was... had a strong bass to it. Maybe it wasn't even Christmas music. I couldn't tell.

The main problem I was having right now was disentangling myself from the cute blonde girl. Tracy? Terry? I couldn't remember her name. She wasn't a patient. She was the daughter of a patient. Her mother had introduced her, then disappeared.

I distinctly remember the mother asking me if I was single

while I cleaned out her ears. And now here I was. Trapped by the daughter. It was a setup.

But I wasn't the least bit interested. I had merely stepped over to the refreshment table to grab three bottles of water when I'd been hijacked.

"Maybe we can go out sometime," she said.

"Sure. Maybe," I said. I saw Bella glance in my direction, then look away. "Sorry," I said. "Mrs. Alexander is waiting for me to bring her this water." I held up the bottle in my left hand and used the moment to escape.

By the time I made my way back to our tree, Bella was standing there staring at the birds or the twinkling lights.

"I brought you some water," I said, standing next to her.

"Thank you." She looked up and blinked, but not before I saw the sadness in her eyes.

"Is there anything else we have to do?" I asked.

She shrugged. "Not that I know of."

"You want to get out of here? Take a walk in the snow?"

She smiled then. She smiled and my heart tripped over itself.

"Come on," I said. "I'll get our coats."

I grabbed our coats from one of the chairs and held hers while she got into it. Then I held out her scarf. Both of us had charcoal gray scarves. Hers was just thicker than mine. Mine had been a gift from Aunt Brianna and had a silky feel to it. "Don't want to forget this."

"No kidding about that."

She wrapped the scarf around her neck, then tugged on her black leather gloves.

"Ready?"

She nodded and we took off toward the door. But it was crowded and I was having trouble keeping up with her.

Finally, I took her hand in mine and we wove our way

through the crowd, finally reaching the door leading to outside.

I should have released her hand. But I just didn't want to. It felt right in mine.

And she didn't try to pull away.

The air was frigid and soft snowflakes lodged in our eyelashes. Bella had layered her scarf over her head to keep her hair from getting soaked.

"Where are we going?" she asked.

"I don't really know." I glanced over at her. Her head was lowered, looking straight down and ahead. "Any suggestions?"

"Somewhere warm," she said, between chattering teeth.

"Home?" I asked, but I really wasn't ready to go home. If we went home, she might go to her room.

She shook her head. "There's a place," she said. "If it's still there."

"What's it called? Maybe I've heard of it."

"The Hungry Hat," she said.

"The what?" With her face all covered up with the scarf I couldn't tell if she was kidding me or not.

"The Hungry Hat."

"I definitely haven't heard of that one. Is it a restaurant?"

"Used to be… and a bar."

"Lead the way," I said.

She stopped and looked around. "This way," she said, tugging my hand and leading me down a side street to the left.

As soon as we stepped inside the door of the restaurant and bar with a huge roaring fireplace, I knew that the Hungry Hat was my new favorite place in Whiskey Springs.

"Table for two?" the hostess asked as we had no more than stepped inside.

Bella glanced at me. "I think we'll just sit by the fireplace first."

"Sure thing," the hostess said. "Wherever you like."

There was a vacant cozy sofa right in front of the fireplace. Definitely my new favorite place.

25

BELLA

$\mathcal{W}$e ordered glasses of rosé wine after we settled on the sofa in front of the fireplace and unbundled.

It wasn't real wood, but the gas logs could have passed for real logs. The flames were certainly warm and that was all that mattered.

There weren't many people here, so it was nicely uncrowded after being in the noisy gym.

The Christmas music in the background wasn't so overbearing that we couldn't hear each other talking.

"This is nice," Jack said. "I'm surprised I haven't heard of it."

I grinned. "One of the benefits of being born and bred."

"I guess so."

He held up his wine glass in a toast. "To Whiskey Springs," he said.

I held my glass near his, then took a sip. I'd never had rosé wine, but since I'd picked the place, I left the wine choice up to him.

It wasn't what I had expected. I'd honestly expected him to

order beer or whiskey or some other typical drink that guys ordered. Rosé wine was… different. Unexpected.

I liked it.

And it was surprisingly good. I told him so.

He grinned. "I thought you might like it. My Aunt Brianna loves it."

"Your aunt?"

This was the first he'd said anything about his family.

"Yeah," he said with a shrug. "She's was something of an Internet phenom. Still is, but she has five children."

"Five children?" I couldn't begin to imagine.

"We have a big family."

"You must miss them," I said, "especially now at Christmastime."

"I do," he said, staring into the fire. "But they all understand. Everybody has their things they do."

"Are you the only doctor in the family?" I asked.

"The only medical doctor," he said. "But we have psychologists."

I blinked. Shook my head a little.

"Say that again," I said.

Frowning, he looked at me, obviously baffled. "I'm the only medical doctor."

"No," I said. "The other thing."

"We have psychologists in the family?"

"Yes. That."

My thoughts were… confused. Jack wasn't who I thought he was.

"You must know a lot about psychology then," I said.

"I know a little," he said, looking unconcerned.

"A little."

"I haven't ruled out psychiatry."

I nodded slowly. "You didn't tell me."

He was holding his wine glass in both hands. "It didn't come up."

"No," I said. "I don't suppose it did."

I took a big swallow of my wine.

It didn't matter.

It didn't matter that he knew a lot about my profession. After all, I knew a lot about his, too. And he didn't seem to be concerned with that.

I sat back against the soft sofa and closed my eyes.

Maybe my coming here hadn't been a good idea.

I was over Anthony. I was.

I wasn't on the rebound.

I could *feel* Jack sitting next to me. He was the kind of guy a girl couldn't not notice.

But this could never work.

I lived in Pittsburg.

He lived here. Or if not here, then Houston or somewhere else.

Relationships were all about proximity.

Humans dated people close to them.

It was a well-accepted fact. It was the only way it could work.

Dr. Jack Fleming could not—would not—be for me.

26

JACK

The warmth of the cozy fire seeped into my skin along with the rosé wine. So I was getting warm from the outside and the inside at the same time.

The fireplace mantle was draped with a twinkling wintry pine garland with cones and red berries.

It matched the Christmas tree near the front of the restaurant. Also decorated with twinkling clear lights and cones and red berries.

The fruity scent of the wine mixed with the tangy scent of the garland, created what could have been a relaxed atmosphere.

But I was far from being relaxed.

Something was going on with Bella.

I could see the emotions as they crossed her features.

For some reason, although I couldn't fathom why, the conversation had stopped when I told her that I had psychologists in the family.

We had a whole bunch of psychologists and pilots and then there were people like me. Anomalies. One medical doctor. An occasional engineer. An architect.

Now that I thought about it, everyone in my family was successful in their own right.

It would have been easy to sit back and let my Grandpa's fortune carry everyone. God knew he had enough money.

Grandpa had taken a single small aircraft, started his own business, and turned it into an empire.

Even now, nearing seventy years old, Grandpa was still going strong. Working on projects. Making more money than he could ever use.

It would all go to us one day. I hoped it would be a really long time before that happened.

My grandfather was one of my favorite people. He and my grandmother both.

I came from a good family. I was a lucky man and I knew it.

Nothing like Bella's family.

It was odd because her parents were likeable. They just didn't seem to know how to be parents.

It made me sad for her.

But despite that, she had turned out well.

Bella sat up and placed her wine glass on the table in front of us.

"I have to go," she blurted.

"What?" She wasn't holding her phone so she hadn't gotten any kind of message. I didn't even know where her phone was.

She stood up, not meeting my gaze.

"I have to go," she said again, grabbing her coat from the chair.

Before I had time to react, she was in her coat and was wrapping her scarf around her.

"What's happened?" I asked, standing in front of her so she couldn't get past me to the door.

"Bella," I said, finally getting her to meet my gaze.

Her moist green eyes were so full of sadness.

I didn't understand.

One minute we were just sitting here talking.

Then the next minute she was running away from me.

"I don't understand," I said. "What did I do wrong?"

"You didn't do anything," she said, her voice barely audible. Her eyes searched mine. "But…" She swallowed. "I can't."

Then she turned and went the other way, turned, and practically ran for the door.

Bewildered, I knew I had to let her go.

But I also knew that I needed to make sure she got home—if that was where she was headed—safely.

Whatever it was I felt an overarching need to fix it.

I didn't want to let her go.

But I had no choice.

27

BELLA

*M*y eyes burned as I tossed clothes into my suitcase.

I pulled out my phone and checked the weather.

I wasn't going anywhere tonight.

The weather conditions were deteriorating by the minute. It wasn't a blizzard exactly, but the conditions were blizzard like.

I was from here. I knew better than to try to travel in conditions like this. Accidents happened in this kind of weather. More so than any other time.

Maybe in the morning. Maybe not. I would have to see.

I sat down hard on the bed and stared out the window at the snow flurries coming down.

I loved this time of year. I even loved it when it snowed, especially at Christmas.

And yet I felt so incredibly sad. So sad and if anyone pressed me to explain why, I wouldn't be able to explain.

I was being rash. Illogical.

But I felt like I had to do something.

I felt like I had to get away from here.

The more time I spent with Jack, the more I liked him.

And liking Jack was just trouble.

Liking Jack wasn't going to get me anywhere.

Except maybe heartbreak.

Unnecessary heartbreak.

I knew better.

I knew not to let myself fall for someone who lived literally across the country.

And I wasn't interested in a holiday romance.

Besides, this wasn't one of those happily-ever-after holiday movies where everything worked out against all odds.

From where I was sitting, the odds were not looking like anything I wanted to put my money on.

The door downstairs opened and I heard my parents talking.

They didn't seem to mind that I was here, but I didn't think they would be particularly unhappy if I left either.

It was a strange position to be in.

I checked the weather again.

Then I checked flights out of Denver tomorrow.

If I could get to Denver, I could get out of here and get home.

That was what I needed to do.

I took a deep breath and put in a request for the flight.

I knew how to drive in the snow. I could get to the airport.

I needed to be back in my world. I did not need to be here, falling for a man who couldn't be.

Jack and I could not happen.

There were too many obstacles.

As I picked up the scarf I had worn home from the Hungry Hat, I realized it wasn't my scarf. The scarf belonged to Jack. In my haste to get away from him, I had grabbed his scarf instead of mine.

I wrapped it around my neck and breathed in his earthy, clean scent.

I liked him.

The acceptance settled over me like a warm blanket.

My phone chimed.

It was a text from the airline. All flights were cancelled out of Denver for tomorrow.

Well. That wasn't what the weather prediction had been.

Then I realized I hadn't checked the Denver weather forecast.

I'd been away from here so long, I'd forgotten just how much different a few miles made in this kind of elevation.

It could be that I just needed to face Jack head on. Running away from him wasn't solving anything anyway.

Maybe, oddly enough, if I talked to him more, I'd like him less.

I smiled to myself.

That happened more often than I cared to think about.

I pulled off his scarf and tucked it between my pillows.

Then I opened my door and headed downstairs.

I just needed a glass of water. At least that was my excuse.

Even as I told myself all this, I knew it was crazy thinking.

There was no way I was going to ever like Jack Fleming any less.

28

JACK

*A*fter following Bella home, from a distance, of course, I turned on the electric tea kettle and sat at the kitchen table while I waited for the water to heat. I thought about making coffee, but the sight of the monstrosity sitting on the kitchen counter struck fear in my heart.

Her parents came inside, but instead of coming into the kitchen, they went straight upstairs. I was a bit relieved because I didn't want them asking about Bella. Not when I couldn't figure out what was going on with her myself.

I was still baffled about what had prompted her to run out of the restaurant. For the life of me, I couldn't figure it out.

I'd replayed our conversation over and over all the way home, but I couldn't come up with anything that could have led her to be so upset that she had to dash away like she was Cinderella and the clock had struck Midnight.

With the water boiling, I got up and made my tea. The mug I chose was red with *Merry Christmas* painted on both sides.

I turned around and nearly spilled it.

Bella was standing there in the doorway looking at me.

She was still wearing her jeans and sweatshirt, but she had

swept her hair to one side. How was it possible that she was more beautiful than she had been the last time I had seen her?

She smiled tentatively at me.

"Is everything okay?" I asked.

She nodded.

"Are you sure? Do you feel sick?"

I hadn't really considered it at the time, but there could be something medically wrong with her.

I felt a little ill myself as I considered some of the possibilities.

Maybe she had migraines. Or, God forbid, maybe she was pregnant.

"I'm okay," she said. "I'm sorry I ran out like that."

"It's okay," I said. "I was just concerned about you. Do you want some tea?"

"Sure," she said.

She sat down at the table while I made her a cup of tea. Her mug was blue with Whiskey Springs painted across the side of it.

It was quiet in the house. With the snow falling outside, we were in our own little cocoon.

I liked it. I would like being snowed in with her. Here or somewhere else would be okay, too.

Maybe a cabin somewhere. With a fireplace that had real logs.

"Here you go," I said, handing her the mug of tea and purposefully stopping my line of thinking.

I knew I was attracted to her, but my thoughts did not need to be going down this path.

She would be leaving soon.

I had to keep reminding myself of that.

"Want to go into the living room?" I asked.

"Good idea."

I put our tea on a tray and led the way.

As we settled on the sofa, she pulled her feet up under her.

She took a sip of tea. Then she just looked at me as though she couldn't quite figure something out.

"You look confused," I said.

"I am," she said with a little smile.

Using the honey bear shaped container, I added some more honey, even though my tea was just fine the way it was.

"Anything I can help with?" I asked.

She smiled a little. "I'm not sure."

"You can try me."

"It's been ten years since I've been here. I'm not so sure I should have even come home now."

"Why's that?" I asked.

She sat back and seemed to consider her words carefully. "My parents have their lives the way they want them. I don't feel right being here."

I bit the inside of my mouth to keep from saying anything. It broke my heart that she thought that way. That a thought like that even crossed her mind.

She looked at me with her beautiful big green eyes. I couldn't sit in silence any longer.

"I've never gotten any indication from them to suggest anything like that."

"It's crazy, isn't it?" she asked, sipping her tea.

"A little maybe," I said. "But I'm not discounting your feelings. I just hate that you feel that way."

"It sounds worse saying it out loud," she said, glancing at me, then staring into the flames. "I'm probably just projecting. Feeling guilty for not coming home for so long."

She was leaning forward, her hands clutching the sofa fabric of the sofa on either side of her. Reaching over, I placed a hand over hers.

She looked up at me with surprise and something that looked suspiciously like resignation.

"You don't have anything to worry about," I said. "Parents are surprisingly resilient. They make it without us just fine."

She smiled at the irony of my statement, her green eyes sparkling from the twinkling lights from the tree in front of the window.

Or maybe they were just sparkling of their own accord.

Either way, they were mesmerizing.

My gaze was pulled to her lips and I couldn't help but wonder.

Maybe it was just the magic of the holidays, but I found myself drawn to her.

Wondering if maybe, just maybe, there might be a way to make things work with her.

29

BELLA

*T*here was something magical about sitting this close to Jack. About having his hand on mine.

I'd known that I would see him if I came downstairs.

I was a strong believer in fate.

Maybe that was why I had stayed away from Whiskey Springs for so long. Maybe I'd known all along that coming back here was risky. That if I did, I could end up liking it or worse, liking it AND someone who lived here.

It didn't even matter that Jack didn't live here, at least not permanently. He was here now. And I felt that pull.

That pull of Whiskey Springs—a place I was finding wasn't really all that bad after all. And most certainly that pull toward Jack.

There was no way I was going to be able to resist him. I recognized this feeling. And through that recognition, I felt something more. Something more powerful.

I was drawn to him.

And how was it possible that the two of us had ended up here, together, at the same time in Whiskey Springs, if not fate?

The twinkling lights from the tree just over in the other room reflected in his smiling eyes. I loved the way his eyes always looked like they were smiling.

He seemed so... happy.

He was someone I wanted to be near. It wasn't just because of his sexy good looks and smiling eyes. It was the way he seemed to always find the positive in things.

It was rather hard to find someone, it seemed, who could do that.

And right now with his hand on mine, all sorts of drunken butterflies were swirling in my stomach.

My gaze drifted to his lips and I felt myself swaying just a little and my eyes were closing.

I could lean forward just a little more and our lips would touch.

"There you are," Daddy said and we both sat up straight. Jack released my hand.

Daddy barreled passed us into the kitchen, not seeming to notice that he had interrupted what could have been a kiss.

Daddy went straight to the kitchen and filled a glass with water.

Jack and I looked at each other with obvious confusion. We didn't know which one of us he had been looking for.

But if I had to guess, I'd guess that he had been looking for Jack.

I couldn't imagine why he would be looking for me.

Jack, on the other hand... there could be any myriad number of reasons he might be looking for Jack.

As Daddy drained his water glass and filled it again, Jack and I just looked at each other.

Then Jack winked at me and everything shifted again.

I was so very falling for him.

And that was something I couldn't possibly run away from.

And, truly, why would I want to?

In the great course of things, this was one of those feelings a person longed to have to run toward.

If I was running from this feeling, then something was most certainly wrong with me.

30

JACK

*A*lthough I had done everything I could to assure Bella that her being here was not disruptive to her parents, I wasn't so sure.

Her mother seemed okay. But her father was acting strange.

As Doc Alexander stood at the sink drinking water from a glass, I looked at Bella.

The only sound besides him filling his glass, was the steady ticking of the grandfather clock in the foyer.

Bella looked bewildered until I winked at her. Then she simply smiled back.

I hadn't planned on winking at her. I didn't wink at people. But it had just happened.

From the look on her face, perhaps I needed to start.

Doc Alexander put his glass in the dishwasher, then walked straight back to face me.

"Mr. Adams out on Highway 28 called in. Complaining of chest pains. You up for a drive? We can take the old truck with the good all weather tires on it."

"Sure," I said. His request did not sound like a request at all.

I looked over at Bella. "See you in the morning?"

"Okay," she said, smiling at me.

Her father made a sound that I couldn't decide was a scoff or a growl. But the expression on his face was most definitely a grimace.

Right now I didn't care.

I'd go with him.

And I'd put up with his bullshit at least to some extent.

No matter what profession I had chosen, one of the benefits of being Noah Worthington's grandson was that I could get another fellowship.

Grandpa's name opened doors.

I had actually never used Grandpa to my advantage. In fact, the Alexanders did not even know that I was related to him, but I wasn't above it.

All that to say, if I had to make a choice between this fellowship and Bella, it was no choice.

I chose Bella.

They said that when a man found the woman he wanted to spend his life with, it was like a bolt of lightning. Every one of my uncles claimed that it had happened to them. Just like that.

They were just going along, minding their own business, when *the girl* walked into their life.

For some of them, it took two chances to get it right, but they all knew without a doubt when they found the love of their life, they knew it, even if they didn't admit it.

Right now, in this moment, I was officially admitting to myself that I had found the woman I was going to marry.

Fate was a funny thing, though. Fate did not make things easy.

Out of all the women in the world, including those who conveniently lived in Houston, I just had to pick this one. This one who lived literally across the country, not only from where I lived right now, but to where I planned on living after I left here. Houston. Where most of my family lived.

A handful of my cousins lived in other states and it looked like I was going to be one of those.

Well. There were worse things.

Right now, one of those worst things was getting in a vehicle with her father.

Nothing induced the same level of fear as the wrath of one's future father-in-law. Especially, perhaps, when he didn't know he was a future father-in-law.

I followed him out to the garage, ignoring the sideways glance he shot me when he caught sight of my secret smile.

31

BELLA

It was two twenty-four when I woke in the night. I know because I picked up my phone from the nightstand and looked at the time.

It was quiet. I strained to hear anything at all in the house. But there was nothing other than the wind whipping around the corner of the house.

Growing up in this room, I'd become very familiar with the sound of that wind.

I rolled over and stared into the darkness in the general direction of the ceiling.

I'd fallen asleep with my cheek on Jack's scarf.

Had he even noticed that he had mine?

I doubted it. They were both gray, after all, and guys didn't typically notice such things.

I wouldn't tell him. I certainly wouldn't tell him that I had slept with it tucked under my cheek. He might think I was weird.

I might switch them back when he wasn't looking. Or I might not.

We would have to see.

Maybe I would keep it as a memento of the man who stole my heart in Whiskey Springs.

I obviously wasn't going back to sleep, so I sat up, pillows behind me, and scrolled my email.

The winter break was an interesting time in academia. Most professors stayed where they were in their jobs. But there were the occasional job openings.

And this year was no different.

It was with idle curiosity that typically led me to open those emails that listed mid-year job postings.

I'd been in the same place since finishing graduate school and had worked my way up to associate professor. That distinction really meant nothing to those outside of the university systems. But it had been enough that I had stayed in the same job.

Most of my colleagues sent out applications to other universities now and then just to test the waters. Maybe stay in practice. Those who knew me encouraged me to do the same.

I had to admit that after my break up with Anthony, I had been tempted to apply to other places. But I had refused to give him the satisfaction of thinking I would leave my job because of him.

But now I was beginning to think that maybe I should stick my toe in the water. See what else was out there.

There were three jobs listed in my area of training. It should not have surprised me, but all three were online only.

I sat up straighter and read the postings carefully.

I'd known that more and more classes were being taught online, but I had not expected to see listings for associate professor that were completely online.

The postings specifically said that relocation was not required.

Interesting.

I checked the time again. It was three thirty. Five thirty on Pittsburg time.

I might as well just get up. I wasn't going to go back to sleep anyway.

I went into the shower and turned on the water. While the water heated up, I picked out a pair of warm sweatpants to wear.

Then I thought about Jack and put the sweatpants back in the drawer. Pulled out a pair of jeans. This was not one of those times to wear slouchy sweatpants.

This was one of those times when it seemed appropriate to wear something casual, but not slouchy.

It was going to be a snowy day, so I put on a long-sleeve red plaid flannel button-down shirt and pulled on a Harvard sweatshirt over it.

I'd gotten the sweatshirt during a visit to Boston two summers ago when I'd met my brother Charlie there. He'd had a conference and I'd joined him for a couple of days.

It had been nice. The only time he and I gotten together since he had left home. In retrospect, we had missed out by not spending time together as adults.

But since our family hadn't been close, it unfortunately wasn't something either one of us had paid more than passing attention to.

At any rate, the heather gray sweatshirt with red lettering was one of my favorites.

After getting dressed, I spent the next few minutes blow drying my hair.

And thinking about Jack.

32

JACK

*M*y walk along Main Street through the snow was brisk.

It would have been one of those perfect mornings to stay inside and drink homemade coffee, but I stayed away from the monstrous machine sitting on the cabinet.

I was one of the few people out and about on the streets, but I was out earlier than most people even thought about getting up. I was actually a little surprised, retrospectively, that the coffee shop was even open. But then, I was learning, that these northwestern states rarely closed for weather-related reason. If they did, they'd be closed for several months out of the year.

The Christmas music on the sidewalks must be left on twenty-four hours. I'd yet to walk down the street without hearing it blasting over the speakers. The twinkling Christmas lights wrapped around every pole and strung across every space, apparently never turned off either.

I carried two cups of hot coffee—vanilla lattes with caramel drizzle, one in each hand, and kept my head down as I walked into the wind.

I had my scarf—Bella's scarf—wrapped around my head, leaving only my eyes exposed.

Buying Bella a latte was unnecessary since she knew how to use her complex coffee machine and might even prefer it. But the gentleman in me had no choice but to bring her one.

I turned off the main road and headed to the Alexander house. Although I'd ordered the coffees extra hot, they would probably have to be microwaved after a walk in this cold.

Reaching the back door, I set the coffee cups on the floor as I removed my gloves long enough to reach into my pocket and shove the key in the lock.

Just ordinary things like opening a locked door were a lot more difficult in this weather. Of course, I was used to valet parking and riding up to my condo in an elevator.

After making my way inside without incident, I stepped into the kitchen only to see Bella standing at the window. She turned around as I came to the door and smiled at me.

She must have been watching me walk up. I was instantly glad I had brought her a coffee. I would have felt like the worst kind of heel coming in with just one for me.

"I brought you something," I said, handing her one of the two identical coffees.

She smiled as she took it from me. "You're going to spoil me."

"Is that such a bad thing?" I asked.

"No," she said, sliding into one of the wooden chairs at the breakfast table.

My gaze slid to her sweatshirt.

Harvard.

My alma mater. Why would she be wearing a Harvard sweatshirt?

She must have seen the expression on my face. "What's wrong?"

I sat down across from her and sipped my coffee. It was surprisingly still hot.

"Harvard," I said, finally. Not much of an answer, but it was all I could manage at this particular moment.

"I visited," she said, keeping her answer pithy as well. "Why?"

I might would have let it go, but she asked why. Now I had to tell her. I couldn't very well start out being dishonest going into a relationship with her. Even if she didn't know that I was planning on going into a relationship with her.

"I have my medical degree from there," I said.

"From Harvard?" she asked, not hiding the surprise in her voice.

"From Harvard," I said, hiding behind my coffee cup.

She sat back and looked at me with a quizzical expression.

"You're kidding?" she said, hopefully.

I shook my head. "I'm not kidding."

"Why didn't you tell me?" she asked.

"It didn't come up."

I could see her thinking. Trying to decide if it actually had come up.

I grinned at her, trying to distract her, hoping that I was right. That it hadn't come up. It was possible I had missed something—

"I'm a little... impressed," she said, although she sounded more surprised than impressed.

I shrugged.

"Where did you do your undergrad work?" she asked.

"Harvard," I answered.

We sat in silence a moment. The grandfather clock in the foyer chimed the hour and the wind howled around the house.

"Shouldn't you be doing your fellowship somewhere at a big hospital?" Her brow was creased.

"I could be," I said.

"Something doesn't add up," she said to herself, not looking at me anymore. She was looking into the distance, probably at nothing.

I just waited.

Then she looked back at me. "Is something wrong with you?"

I laughed, nearly spitting out my coffee.

"Probably," I said with a little nod.

"What?"

Since she was peering at me with serious concern, I decided to stop kidding and be truthful.

"I chose Whiskey Springs to experience a small practice. In case that's what I decide I wanted to do."

"What do think you want to do?"

"I haven't decided yet. Maybe a small practice. Maybe even psychiatry." It felt a little strange saying it out loud. But I was determined to tell her the truth.

"Okay," she said, stretching her hands out on the table. "Let me see if I understand."

"Okay."

"You were born and raised in Houston."

I nodded.

"Then you went to college at Harvard in Boston."

I nodded again.

"But with your coveted degree, you came to Whiskey Springs to do your fellowship."

"Pretty good summary," I said.

She looked at me with obvious skepticism.

This wasn't going exactly as I had planned.

33

BELLA

*T*he steady ticking of the grandfather clock was the only sound until the refrigerator cut on adding its steady roar to the background noise.

I took a sip of the latte Jack had brought me. He seemed determined not to use the coffee maker on the counter. Not that I was complaining. The coffee shop coffees were always better.

I'd thought he didn't use it because he had never been around anything like it.

Now I didn't know what to think.

The man had gone to college and med school at Harvard. The best medical school in the country.

It just did not add up.

I was missing a piece of information about him, but I didn't know enough to ask the right question to find out what that piece of information was.

Since he came from a big family, I had just made the assumption that his family struggled for money. But... Harvard...

It would be rude to ask if he had scholarships.

So I didn't ask.

Instead, I changed the subject.

"I'm glad you made it back from your trip with my father in one piece," I said.

"It wasn't bad," he said. "Mr. Adams was having a panic attack."

"Oh," I said, not knowing what else to say.

I couldn't ask him what he and my father talked about. That would be rude, too.

We'd had no trouble talking to each other yesterday. It was like a wall had gone up between us. And all because I wore my Harvard sweatshirt.

Fortunately, our misery didn't last long. My mother swept into the kitchen.

"Oh good," she said. "You're both here. Can either of you spare some time to help me make cookies for the North Pole Express tonight?"

"You're making the cookies?" I asked. "I thought the Daniels made those." I knew that my protest was feeble. Anytime my mother asked for help, I knew that she wasn't actually asking. She was telling us that we were going to help her.

"Not sure they can get here," Momma said, pulling bowls out of the cabinet and ingredients from the cupboard.

The Daniels lived several miles higher in elevation up a private blacktop road. They lived in what everyone called a castle in the sky. I'd been there once. Breathtaking views.

Momma set a carton of eggs on the counter. Apparently, she meant we were making cookies right now.

"I can help," Jack said.

Now I had to help to keep from looking bad.

"Good," Momma said. "Help me clear off the table."

Jack and I looked at each other. There was nothing on the table to clear off other than our coffee cups.

"Psychiatry could be an interesting thing to study," I said.

Jack hid a laugh.

And just like that, we were back to normal.

"We'll make sugar cookies using these cookie cutters," Momma said, setting a tattered cardboard box, about the size of a shoe box, on the table. I recognized the box and realized that it was actually a shoe box. A really old shoe box.

I recognized the cookie cutters, too. They were the same ones we'd used when I was growing up.

"These look familiar," I said, sorting them. A snowman. A Santa. A tree. All the usual cookie cutters.

"Some things stay the same," Jack said. "Nothing wrong with that."

"I guess." There he was. Being positive again.

Jack was a good guy.

And I wouldn't mind having him around. All the time.

I glanced at him from beneath my lashes.

I wondered what he would think if he knew the direction of my thoughts.

I couldn't tell him, of course. That was one of the quickest ways to lose a guy.

34

JACK

I quickly learned that Bella only ate cookies in the shape of bells and balls. Maybe, if pressed, a tree. Because she didn't want to bite the head off of snowmen or Santas or even reindeer.

I found it endearing.

We'd made about two dozen cookies when Mrs. Alexander had to take a phone call. Apparently, the wife of the town's primary physician, even almost retired primary physician, had lots of social duties.

"What should we make next?" I asked Bella after her mother had disappeared down the hall with her phone to her ear.

"I don't think we're going to make anything," she said. "We're out of cookie dough."

"And when did that become a problem?" I asked.

"Well..."

"Are you telling me Professor Bella Alexander that you don't know how to make cookie dough?"

"I know where to buy it," she said, biting her lip.

I shot her a mock look of horror.

"I can't believe that a girl from the Christmas town of Whiskey Springs doesn't know how to make cookie dough."

"Hey," she said. "I have other skills."

"Like what?"

Our gazes met a moment and neither one of us said anything.

Then she broke the silence. "I can string popcorn like a champ."

"Popcorn, huh? Well. We'll have to see about that."

She grinned.

"But first," I said. "You can be my assistant."

With an exaggerated flourish, I held out my right hand, palm up. "Egg," I said.

With a little laugh, she placed an egg in my hand. I broke it and deftly dropped it into the bowl. Tossing the shell in the disposal. Then held out my hand again. "Another egg."

"Are you sure, Doctor?" she asked.

"You have to trust me on this," I said, in my sternest voice.

She put another egg in my hand. I added it to the first one.

Then I held out my hand again. "One cup of flour," I said.

She dipped the measuring cup into the bag of flour and came out with a cup full. She moved a little too fast, though, ending up with flour dusting across her nose and her cheeks.

She handed me the cup. I dumped it in the bowl, then turned back and locked my gaze on hers.

"What's nex—"

In one swift movement, I closed the small distance between us, used one finger to lightly follow the dusting of powder across her right cheek, and cupped her head with both hands.

Then I placed my lips against hers and just held.

She tasted like cookie dough and flour and… heaven.

I wanted to stay right here, like this, my lips pressed against hers until the end of time.

Then she kissed me back.

And I was a lost man.

Lured over the rocks by the siren's song and lost forever.

I wasn't going anywhere else other than right here.

Somewhere along the way, Bella Alexander had stolen my heart, all in the blink of an eye.

35

BELLA

*T*here were some things a girl knew she would never forget.

Like the first kiss by the man she was falling in love with.

Of course, I'd fancied myself in love before. More than a few times. Anthony came to mind, but I quickly abolished his memory and didn't expect to have any more trouble with it returning.

The wind howled against the window, bringing with it shards of hail.

It was going to be a worse storm than they had predicted.

I was grateful I hadn't tried to travel in this storm.

But being here, sheltering from the storm, wasn't the real reason I was thankful I had stayed.

Right now there was a storm raging through my emotions.

Jack's hands gently cupped the sides of my face, his lips pressed against mine.

The world shifted beneath me.

Life was never going to be the same again. Of that I was certain.

His kiss was perfect.

So perfect I felt my knees weaken and wobble a bit.

Just when I lost all my ability to think, he pulled back and smiled into my eyes.

The hail continued to slam against the window just as my heart pounded against my chest.

"I always did like a good storm," he said, sweeping a lock of hair off my cheek and tucking it behind an ear.

"You don't know anything about snowstorms," I said, teasingly. "You're from Houston."

"But I know all about thunderstorms," he said. "And they're a whole lot louder."

I nodded.

I heard Momma walking back this way. Heard her footsteps after she disconnected the call.

Jack and I decided to take a step back at the same time.

Still smiling at me, he held out his palm again. "Spoon," he said.

With my heart racing, I handed him a wooden spoon.

"I'm glad to see you two are making progress," she said, quickly surveying the situation. Then she grabbed her coat from the coat rack and shrugged into it.

"I have to run downtown for a few minutes," she said.

"In this weather?" I asked.

"It's a short walk," she said.

"I'll walk with you," Jack said, setting the spoon down.

"It's a short walk," Momma said, waving him off. "Don't you dare leave Bella alone with those cookies."

"Yes ma'am," he said.

As she walked out the door, he looked at me. "Should I follow her? Make sure she gets wherever she's going?"

I shook my head. "She'll be fine."

But just offering to go with her had given Jack major points in my book. I knew my mother would be fine. She was born and bred in this kind of weather, but it told me that Jack was a gentleman.

"I don't mind," he said.

"Are you trying to get away from me already?" I asked.

"Not on your life," he said, picking up the spoon. "But I have a feeling that if your mother comes back and doesn't see several dozen cookies baked and ready, she'll have our hide."

"I think you might be right," I said, watching him stir the cookies dough.

I wanted more kissing more than I wanted anything right now.

But the kissing would have to wait.

36

JACK

I'd had a taste of Bella Alexander now and she was all I could think about.

We worked side by side, making the cookies, stealing glances at each other like teenagers.

The hail continued to pelt against the windows and the wind howled around the house. It sounded like a regular storm —the kind I was used to—except that there was no thunder.

It felt like there should have been thunder. It was like a muted storm. I didn't count the sound of the hail pelting against the window.

Doc was down the hall. Another reason for me to keep my hands in the cookie dough and off of Bella. It wouldn't pay to have him catch me with my hands on his daughter. Even if we were both adults.

Didn't make one bit of difference. We were in his house and I had a great deal of respect for the man. And on top of that, technically this was my work place.

Besides, he had some unfounded concerns about Bella that had nothing to do with her and everything to do with his own baggage.

Bella handed me the green food coloring.

"Green again?" I asked.

"We need more trees," she said, sitting down at the table with a pouch of icing to decorate one of the freshly baked tree cookies.

"We ran out of trees because we ate them."

She grinned up at me. "The breakfast of champions."

"A whole lot different from yesterday's breakfast." Yesterday she had made bacon and eggs.

"Just a little." She shrugged. Then she grinned up at me, sending my heart into a spin that was anatomically impossible. "This is a whole lot more fun though, isn't it?"

"Haven't had this much fun since—" I stopped. Looked at her and couldn't resist teasing her. "Since the Houston Astros won the World Series."

She rolled her eyes up. "I feel so special."

I laughed. "In my family, that's a compliment of the highest order."

"Big baseball fans?" she asked.

"Some of my family. I'm not really big into sports."

"Me either."

I grinned at her. "We have that in common."

She outlined a red star at the top of the green cookie tree. "If you go into psychiatry, we'll have even more in common."

"I understand psychology and psychiatry are a lot different from each other." I washed my bowl, getting ready for the next batch of cookies.

"They're distant cousins," she said. "Did you just wash that?"

"Wash what?"

"That bowl? Aren't you about to make another batch?"

I looked down at the clean bowl. "Right," I said. "Bad habit. Keeping everything clean between patients."

She grinned up at me. "Not bad as far as habits go."

"What's your worst habit?" I asked.

She set down her pouch of red icing and picked up a white one. After a moment of obvious consternation, she blinked up at me. "I know you didn't just ask me that."

"Why not?" I asked. "You know mine."

"But yours is a good habit," she said, the pouch forgotten in her hands.

"Maybe yours is a good bad habit, too."

She concentrated on outlining the tree limbs in white.

"Daydreaming," she said.

"Daydreaming what?"

"Daydreaming is my bad habit."

"There," I said. "See. Daydreaming is a good thing."

"I know," she said. "But I daydream when I'm not supposed to."

"Like when?" I asked, breaking an egg and tossing the shell into the garbage disposal.

"Oh," she said. "Like during faculty meetings and sometimes even during movies."

I laughed. "You're such a renegade."

"What are you going to do with me?" she asked.

It was a simple question. A playful question.

But I couldn't help but wonder if the question was coming from a serious place.

I sort of hoped it was. I hoped she was thinking about us beyond this moment.

Because I certainly was.

37

BELLA

*I*t was hard to concentrate on decorating cookies when Jack was right there and all I could think about was that kiss.

He glanced at me while he stirred the cookie dough. Why was there something universally sexy about a man who knew his way around the kitchen?

I think I would have found Jack sexy no matter what he'd been doing.

Someone, a patient, came in the front door, my father greeted them, and led them down to his office.

"Daddy's got early appointments," I said.

"Probably Mr. Adams," he said. "Doc told him to come in first thing this morning to do some tests on his heart."

I looked at Jack with a sick feeling in the pit of my stomach. "He just left him there, last night, banking on it being—hoping — a panic attack?"

"Your father was certain. I think he was using it as an excuse to get Mr. Adams in for a checkup. Apparently that's a hard thing to do."

"Oh," I said, with relief. "Well that makes sense."

I knew my father was a good doctor. But seeing him through Jack's eyes had me questioning the simplest things.

I didn't know much about Jack, but he had to be a good physician, too. He couldn't come out of Harvard medical school and not be. Besides, I could just tell.

And, yes, I was biased now that we'd kissed, but I'd already known he was a good physician BEFORE he kissed me.

"Did you agree with him?" I asked, mostly just out of curiosity.

"I did," Jack said, rolling out the cookie dough and going to the sink to wash the cookie cutters. The cutters he was about to use again.

"You want some more coffee?" I asked.

"Sure."

I went to the coffee maker and fired it up.

"You want me to teach you how to use this?" I asked.

"No way," he said, pressing one of the cookie cutters into the dough. "That thing is terrifying."

I laughed as I added some milk. "What's terrifying about it?"

"Everything," he said. "It looks like something that should be in the surgical room."

I looked at the coffee machine I had been so impressed with.

"So... you just use an old-fashioned coffee machine?"

The wind had stopped howling and the hail had stopped hitting the glass. Now the snowflakes were falling down like silent rain drops.

"Something like that," he said, not meeting my gaze.

I felt like I had stumbled upon a piece of the Jack puzzle, but I didn't know what to do with it.

It would all fit together eventually.

It always did.

Glancing over at the refrigerator, I saw the calendar reminding me that tonight was the Whiskey Springs train ride.

"Since we're making all these cookies for the train ride tonight," I said. "We should probably go."

Jack glanced up at me. "Is that your way of asking me to go on the train ride with you?"

I smiled as I handed him a cup of coffee. "Maybe," I said.

By when his fingers brushed mine, my breath hitched, taking the steam out of my flirty response.

Maybe I should have Jack check my heart, too.

Right now, it was beating at a dangerously fast rate.

38

JACK

*I*t was strange to me, as a southern boy, how the bad weather did not keep people inside.

Where I was from, if the weatherperson merely mentioned the word snow, everything closed down.

Not here in Whiskey Springs. If anything, the snow seemed to bring people out.

Of course, it was also two days before Christmas and the little town was well into its festivities.

The big, vintage narrow-gauge train was mostly for children, but they let adults ride, too.

Other than the tall, lanky teenage boy wrapped around his girlfriend in front of us, we were the tallest people standing in line to buy tickets. Parents, it seemed, trusted their children, the older ones anyway, to buy their own tickets. Most of the younger children, with their parents, already had tickets.

The cold seemed to seep right down to the bone. If I'd been a little bit younger and less of a man who was supposed to comport himself in an exemplary professional fashion, I would have pulled Bella into my arms like the teenager in front of us.

Instead, I linked my gloved fingers lightly with hers and

smiled to myself when she didn't resist. Instead, she squeezed my fingers.

As we made our way to the counter, I felt Bella tense at my side. I took a step, but she didn't.

I turned to see what had her frozen on the spot.

Mrs. Alexander, so bundled up she was barely recognizable, was walking in our direction with a woman about her age and another woman about Bella's age. From what I could tell, which wasn't much considering the scarves wrapped around their head, I'd guess mother and daughter. They moved the same way. With purpose and ease.

While the trio approached, I went ahead and bought our tickets.

By the time I turned around, they were standing in front of Bella. I went to Bella's side and looked questioningly at Mrs. Alexander, but her attention was on her daughter.

I wouldn't have thought much about it, except that Bella's brow was furrowed and the tension flowing through her was palpable.

"Bella," Mrs. Alexander said. "I'd like you to meet your aunt."

Bella's eyes widened, but otherwise she showed no reaction.

"Your Aunt Rebecca," Mrs. Alexander said. "And her daughter, your cousin, Maribelle."

"It's so nice to meet you," Maribelle said, a big smile on her face, holding out her hand toward Bella.

Bella automatically put her hand in her cousins. I looked from one of them to the other. Maribelle and Bella. I tried, but I couldn't see the resemblance. Maribelle was blonde and perky whereas Bella was brunette and serious.

Some of my cousins resembled each other and some did not. So I didn't see that as a problem.

Bella looked from her cousin to her aunt and back. "How?" she asked, swallowing thickly. "How did you get here?"

"We flew into the new airport," Aunt Rebecca said.

"Right," Bella said. "I'd forgotten about that."

I hadn't forgotten about it. My grandfather was behind building the whole thing. But, of course, I couldn't say anything unless I wanted to give away my identity.

Not that I had a problem with anyone knowing I was part of the Worthington clan. It was just at the moment I was content to prove to myself that I could go it on my own.

Then Bella turned and looked at me. "This is Dr. Jack Fleming," she said.

Then she did something that surprised me completely. She linked her arm with mine in what could only be construed as a very possessive move.

A grin spread across my face. I liked it.

39

BELLA

here was an indisputable excitement in the air. It was the day before Christmas Eve and children were bouncing around with excitement about riding the open-air train.. The track only took about thirty minutes to travel around the outside of town, but to them it was a trip to the north pole—to see Santa.

There was Christmas music in the background, but I couldn't really hear it. I couldn't hear anything other than the roar of the old vintage steam engine and the excited squeals of the children as they stood in line preparing to board the train.

The snow had stopped falling as though solely for the purpose of this event.

"All aboard." Somehow the loud voice of the conductor overrode all the other sounds as he removed the red velvet rope keeping everyone back from the train. "Boarding now for the Whiskey Springs North Pole Express."

The younger children jumped up and down with excitement while the older ones tried to stay calm, cool, and collected.

"We're going to ride the train," I blurted.

"Of course," Aunt Rebecca said. "We don't want to interrupt. We were just on our way to find your father and saw you standing here. I wanted to meet you."

"I'm glad you did," I said, recovering somewhat from my shock at meeting the aunt and cousin I had only heard about. For them to be here now was… unexpected and surreal.

"They're staying at our house," Momma said. "Come on home after the train ride and we can all talk."

"Of course." I blew out a breath as they walked off.

"Is that the aunt…?" Jack asked, his voice trailing off.

"Yes," I said. "The mystery aunt who was supposed to have been ruined forever."

"Ruined? Your father didn't give me details."

I waited until we were on the train, then kept my voice to a whisper as I explained.

"She got pregnant in high school. It was such a scandal."

"I see," he said. "I guess that was back in the Victorian days."

I laughed a little. "Not quite, but almost. About the same thing, I guess."

"Unfortunate."

"She went away and no one saw her again."

"She looked quite well considering," Jack said, looking through the crowd as though to catch another glimpse of my mysterious new relatives. "And happy to be here."

"Well, I don't see how. With a ghost in the closet like that, my family wanted nothing more than to bury that memory. And I always assumed she would, too. It had to be why she never came back here."

"It makes sense now," Jack said.

I looked up at him. "How so?"

"It makes sense why your father was so funny about you."

I blinked at him.

The conductor came by and insisted that everyone put their arms inside the train car. I don't know why. There was nothing anywhere near the train. Maybe it was just part of the whole experience.

"You seem to know more about that than I do."

"Your father wouldn't let you date until you were sixteen, right?"

It was snowing again and I shivered. I don't know if it was from the snow or from thinking back to my teenage years.

"How did you know that?" I asked, looking at him sideways.

"Your father mentioned it."

"Well." I sat back against the iron seat. "I actually started dating when I was fifteen."

He nodded. "Your mother's influence?"

"He told you that, too?"

"Didn't have to. It just seems logical."

I grabbed hold of the side of the open car as the train started moving.

Meeting my aunt and cousin had me out of sorts. It wasn't something I had expected and I wasn't very fond of surprises.

Here I was nearly thirty years old and I had just met my father's sister for the first time. And her daughter, my cousin.

I'd heard about the scandal and I had honestly never expected to meet them. Oddly enough, I had been okay with that. My aunt's scandal had created problems in my life and had even caused my relationship with my father to be strained. I hadn't given my aunt much thought since I left home and although I had resented her as a teen, most of the resentment had faded along with any fleeting thoughts I might have of her. It was easy since my parents never talked about her.

In fact... I couldn't remember it ever coming up in conversation that my aunt had given birth to a daughter. It was almost as if when my aunt left home, she ceased to exist.

But now she was here.

I'd had plans for the evening that did not involve my aunt or my cousin or even my parents for that matter.

I'd been planning on having a glass of wine and sitting in front of the fireplace with Jack.

"You okay?" Jack asked.

"Just caught off guard," I said.

He put an arm around me and squeezed, giving me a kiss on the cheek.

"It's a beautiful evening," he said.

I took a deep breath and met his gaze. His beautiful smiling blue eyes locked onto mine.

He was right. It was a beautiful evening and there was no reason to let anyone ruin it.

Then, as the engine chugged, carrying us around the outer part of town, as though on cue, it started to snow again. Big fluffy flakes, drifting down and landing on my sleeves. On my eyelashes.

The bright winter moon lit our way as the train wound its way back toward the high school gym where the children would get to sit on Santa's lap and tell him their secret wish list for Christmas.

It was, I realized, Whiskey Spring's version of a one horse open sleigh.

And there beneath the moonlight, in the falling snow, with twinkling Christmas lights all around us as we neared my old high school gym, Jack kissed me.

40

JACK

*I*t was the night before Christmas Eve, a full moon, snow falling quietly, and so far it was the strangest Christmas I had ever experienced.

My family was big and boisterous. Loud and loving.

The Alexanders were a small family, but having Doc's estranged sister and niece here as unexpected guests added a tension to the air that a person could cut with a knife.

On the surface, everything was friendly and happy. We all sat in the living room with the sparkly, twinkling tree lights as background.

The fire in the fireplace cast a warmth across the room. The four red stockings hanging from the mantle were a reminder of the family's distance from each other. Her brother Charlie's stocking was there, but he wasn't.

Doc Alexander popped a bottle of champagne and poured a glass for everyone.

"To family," he said, holding up his glass in a toast.

It didn't take long though before we began to pair off.

I sat with Bella on the loveseat, closest to the fireplace.

Doc and his sister sat on the other side of the room, deep in conversation.

And Mrs. Alexander chatted quietly with Maribelle.

Aunt Rebecca glanced over at Bella, but Bella didn't see. I tried to keep Bella engaged in conversation so she wouldn't be involved in whatever discussions were going on.

I don't think her parents even realized how much consternation Rebecca and Maribelle showing up was causing her.

"What did your family usually do on Christmas Eve?" I asked, leaning close to Bella.

This was not how I had hoped to spend the evening. I had hoped to spend it right here on this little sofa, but I was hoping it would be just the two us of.

She shrugged. "I don't know. Usually we went to the town Christmas Eve dance."

"Right," I said. "That's so different from what I'm used to."

"I know. Most people get together as a family. But not Whiskey Springs." She took a sip of her champagne.

I quickly changed direction.

"We usually get together as a family. Our family is so big, it's probably a lot like the town of Whiskey Springs getting together."

She laughed. "It can't be that many people."

"Probably not," I said. "But sometimes it seems like it."

"Everyone gets along?"

"We're one big happy family," I said. "Only the occasional rift."

"I can only imagine," she said with a little smile.

I had a feeling there was no way she could possibly imagine my family together in my grandparents' house. First of all, their house was huge. Second, there were so many of us.

And we had so much fun together.

She nodded, her expression somber. Her eyes were misty.

"Then on Christmas Day," I said, changing the subject again. "everyone spends the day with their individual families."

"That sounds like a good way to do it," she said.

"When someone gets married, they're expected to form their own family and traditions, especially if they have children."

She shifted a bit uncomfortably.

And I wondered.

I wondered if she wanted children. If she planned on having a family someday.

And I wondered if maybe she would be willing to move her someday up to sometime soon.

Now that I had found her, I found that I didn't want to wait.

I wanted to get started on our life together.

But I was getting ahead of myself.

Way ahead of myself.

41

BELLA

*I*t was almost ten o'clock, Midnight on Pittsburgh time, when everyone started heading upstairs for bed.

No one had interrupted my conversation with Jack. It seemed my parents were busy catching up with my dad's estranged sister.

The little bits of conversation that I caught, sounded like they were all getting along just fine. They were laughing and having a grand time. I found that surprising since as far as I knew they hadn't spoken to each other for over thirty years. I could be wrong about that, of course. Perhaps my father had been in touch with his sister over the years or at least recently. It wasn't like Daddy and I talked about anything of any substance.

"Are you tired?" Jack asked as I tried to hide a yawn.

I quickly shook my head. "No. Not at all."

He laughed. "It's okay," he said. "I'm tired, too. Want to meet for breakfast in the morning?"

"Eggs or trees?"

"Whatever you prefer. Or..." He looked at me with a

sideways grin. "How about I make you breakfast?"

I grinned. "That sounds like a treat."

"I'll surprise you."

"Do you want me to make you coffee?"

"Maybe," he said. "Let's see how the morning goes."

"Deal." We went to the kitchen for a glass of water.

Daddy stood at the kitchen sink, looking outside.

He looked at us over his shoulder, then turned around.

He had that expression that suggested something was bothering him.

"You okay?" I asked.

"I need to talk to you for a few minutes." His gaze flicked from me to Jack and back again.

"I was just heading up to bed," Jack said, taking his glass with him.

I watched as he walked away, then turned back to my father. I wasn't sure how I felt about him leaving me like this. I suppose he was being respectful giving me some time with my father, but I would have preferred that he stay.

I squared my shoulders. That was messed up. He was my father and I shouldn't be nervous about talking to him.

"Have a seat," he said, pulling out a chair, then sitting across from it.

I didn't remember him being such a gentleman. It rather caught me off guard. Maybe Momma's talk of me finding a gentleman had something to do with Daddy.

Of course, I hadn't seen him in ten years. Not really. Not counting Facetime.

He had some wrinkles around his eyes I hadn't noticed before and his hair was most definitely going gray.

I swallowed the lump in my throat.

I'd missed time.

I'd missed time with my parents that I couldn't get back. And the truth was, I really couldn't even explain what had started the whole thing. And I certainly couldn't explain why it had gone on so long.

It had somehow turned into a pattern. And the pattern had just taken on a life of its own.

"I'm glad you finally got to meet my sister," Daddy said and I could hear the emotion in his voice.

"Me too," I said. "Did you know she was coming?"

"Not for sure," he said, looking toward the window where the snow was starting to pile up on the glass. "I didn't know she had access to a private jet."

"I guess not."

My family did well enough, but not private jet well. Being the physician in a small town carried more prestige than money. And college professors certainly didn't fall into the private jet class.

"But it's late and this isn't about her."

"Oh?"

"Not really. It's more about you. About us."

Now I was feeling nervous. Having a heart-to-heart with my father was unexpected to say the least and I wasn't the least bit prepared.

"I owe you an apology."

"For what?"

"When my sister got pregnant, it was a devastating scandal." He took a breath. "Especially for me. She was five years older. And when she left... I... I lost her."

Daddy was telling me things I'd never known and had never even known to think about.

"I'm sorry," I said, not knowing what else to say.

"I was a child. Twelve years old. There was nothing I could do about it," he said. "But I never should have taken that helplessness out on you."

"I don't understand."

He shook his head and looked away. "I didn't want the same

thing to happen to you. I didn't want to lose you, too." He turned and looked into my eyes. "But by holding on too tight, I lost you anyway."

I reached out. Put a hand over his. "You didn't lose me, Daddy. I'm here now."

"All those years," he said.

My eyes filled with tears and I couldn't speak past the lump in my throat.

"Will you forgive a foolish old man?"

I got up, went around the table, and hugged him.

"There's nothing to forgive," I said. "I was as much at fault as you were. And we're here together now."

"Yes," he said. "And just so you know, I like Jack. I like him a lot."

I dropped into the chair next to him.

"Good," I said. "I like him, too."

He nodded. "I'm hoping he'll stay in Whiskey Springs. Take over my practice."

"Really?" I looked over my shoulder as though expecting Jack to be standing there listening. "Do you think he will?"

"I think it's possible that he just might. But it might take some convincing from you."

"Me?" Convincing from me could mean a lot of things, but right now, I could only think of one thing.

He shrugged. "You can't fault a father for trying."

No. I couldn't fault him for trying.

Especially when he was right.

42

JACK

I got up a little bit earlier than usual the next day.

Today was Christmas Eve. In my family, Christmas Eve was the most magical time of year.

And as such, I wanted to do something to bring some magic to Bella.

The first order of business was a quick walk to the coffee shop.

I'd barely stepped out the back door before I was already questioning the decision to buy coffee.

She'd offered to make it with her monstrous coffee machine contraption and I should have let her.

The cold sliced through me, straight through my coat and scarf and gloves.

As I walked beneath the street lights with the snow falling like sparkling rain, I decided the walk was worth it.

The falling snow was beautiful.

And I didn't know what the next year would bring. Didn't know where I would be.

So I knew to enjoy the moment.

No matter what happened, I would have this memory.

It snowed in Pittsburgh, too.

The thought should not have surprised me. I was getting accustomed to my heart sending me little messages involving Bella.

No matter how pretty the view, I stepped into the coffee shop with relief and a deep breath as the warmth swept over me.

Bella was standing there at the pickup counter. She stood, looking quite serene, bundled in her long gray coat, her hands in her pockets, and her scarf draped loosely over her shoulders.

Every cell in my body went on alert. I blinked, wondering for a split second if I had perhaps somehow conjured her up.

"Good morning," she said with a smile.

I quickly recovered. "You beat me at my own game."

"I thought I would surprise you," she said, her bow-shaped lips curved into a secret looking smile. But I didn't have time to process that.

"Bella," the barista called her name as she set two festive green paper coffee cups on the counter.

Bella took the coffees and handed one to me.

"If I could figure out how to make coffee like this at home, wouldn't life be so much better?" she asked as we took a seat at one of the little tables.

Yes, I thought. And I could do just that with a mere press of a button in my condo. Maybe not quite as good, but a passing approximation.

We were the only customers in the coffee shop and there were only two workers behind the counter.

As the sound of the coffee grinder filled the room, we sat in silence.

Finally, it stopped and was replaced by the softer sound of the steamer and clink of metal against metal as the workers went about their business.

"You hungry?" I asked. "Want a muffin?"

"Maybe in a few minutes," she said.

I sipped my coffee and watched her. Something seemed to be troubling her.

"Everything go okay with your father last night?" I asked.

I wasn't sure if I should bring it up, but it seemed like something needed to be said. I knew that she'd been distant from her family over the years.

With the unexpected appearance of her aunt, the same aunt that started the whole thing years ago, I could only imagine what Bella might be struggling to process.

"It was good," she said, sipping her coffee. "Really good."

"Yeah?"

"Yeah," she said, her brow creasing a little. "He apologized to me. And explained what had happened. How he'd lost his sister and didn't want to lose me, too."

I put a hand over hers. "I'm so happy for you."

"Me too."

"How do you feel now?"

"I have some regret," she admitted on a little sigh. "But also hope going forward." I could see that hope as she looked at me from beneath her wonderfully dark, thick eyelashes.

I looked around the coffee shop and reflected that I didn't feel that same level of hope that she did.

I was starting to think about her leaving and I hated that. I was usually pretty good at staying in the moment, but for some reason, I wasn't able to do that with Bella.

A young man in his early twenties who looked like he was on his way to a banking job walked in and ordered a coffee. It was funny how just having one other customer changed the whole feel of the coffee shop. When it was just the two of us, the workers doing their own thing, fading into the background, it had felt almost like we were in her parents' kitchen.

I looked back at Bella. Her skin was still flushed a bit from the cold, but her eyes looked brighter than they had since I'd met her. It was a good thing, her talking with her father.

I couldn't get enough of her. That was the problem. If I could just keep her here… or go with her…

Long distance relationships didn't work. I knew that. And thinking about it was like a stab in my heart. Maybe I'd become a pilot instead of a doctor, it might have worked. But…

"Daddy said something else," she said.

43

BELLA

*G*etting up before daylight and walking through the snow to the coffeeshop had been a crazy idea.

But it was Christmas Eve and it just felt right.

Besides, I enjoyed the walk by myself in the cold snowy predawn morning.

There was something magical about snow falling on blue Spruce trees. It was like nature's way of decorating for Christmas. It might not seem like that in January, but today, on Christmas Eve, it did. It was magical.

I'd thought I would be home before Jack got up and came downstairs, but it seemed he had the same idea I did.

My talk with Daddy had shifted something in my brain. I felt freer than I could ever remember feeling.

The unspoken conflict with my parents had been like a weight on my shoulders. And now it wasn't there.

That was part of it. Jack was the other part.

I liked him.

I liked him even though I knew there was no way that we could work.

We lived too far apart. And I knew all about the importance

of proximity in relationships. I taught it to my students, for God's sake.

But I had my father's blessing. And that wasn't nothing.

I'd never had that before.

Not once when I'd lived at home and dated boys in high school. After I left home, I hadn't talked to my family about boyfriends.

So those ten years were just a blur. It was almost like they never happened.

It was so very odd and so very insane. And so very comforting.

But sitting here with Jack, I couldn't think of anywhere I would rather be.

I'd never been in a relationship that felt so easy. That just seemed to fall into place. We'd never been on a date. He'd never taken me to dinner and a movie.

And yet none of that mattered.

I was falling for him anyway. All that dating stuff meant nothing. It had nothing to do with how two people felt about each other. We, as a society, just pretended that it did. The dates. The flowers. The gifts. Those were just things we used to measure relationships. But after those things were done, people were left with the bare bones of what it meant to be in a relationship.

Jack and I had simply skipped all the pretenses that came with traditional dating. We'd skipped it and gone straight to the things that mattered.

It helped that he already knew my parents and they knew him. He actually knew my parents better than I did at this point.

A clean-cut, handsome young man wearing a long woolen coat and a little stylish hat, who looked like he belonged in a city, not here in Whiskey Springs came into the coffee shop and ordered a coffee and a muffin.

I found myself wondering if Jack and I looked like we belonged here. I liked to think we did. I liked to think that we would fit in anywhere we chose to go.

"What else did your father say?" Jack asked, jarring my attention back to him.

"You know he's retiring," I said.

"Of course."

This felt like a rather intimate conversation to be having with someone I'd only met a couple of days ago.

I took a deep breath and just spit it out, trying to make it sound normal. Matter-of-fact. As though Daddy had told me that he was thinking of buying a new truck. Which he did need to do, by the way. "He mentioned that he'd like you to take over his practice."

To my relief, Jack did not seem the least bit surprised or even taken aback.

"I know," he said. "He talked about it to me."

"Oh. Right. Of course." I watched the young man take his coffee and muffin and sit two tables over. "But you don't know what you want to do just yet."

"I have mixed feelings," he said.

"I can only imagine. It's quite different living here from living in Houston."

When he didn't answer, I added. "You'll want to live here for at least a year before you make that kind of decision. Go through all the seasons."

My suggestion was rational and logical. And yet... here I was falling in love with someone I had only known a couple of days. Didn't falling in love merit the same kind of deliberate thought and exploration as a change of career?

"I'll order us some muffins," he said, starting to stand up, then stopped. "You like muffins or do you want a scone? Or I think they have some kind of biscuit thing."

I smiled. "A muffin is fine," I said.

As I watched Jack go to the counter and order muffins, I realized that the answer to my own question was quite simply no. Falling in love required the opposite of deliberation.

Deliberation could kill it.

My aunt had fallen in love at seventeen. And even though she had not married the father of her child right away, she had gotten back with him two years later when they were no longer governed by the adults in their lives.

They were still happily married. Their teenage hearts had known.

The heart knew.

If we took the time to look deep, to get away from what society expected of us, the heart always knew.

And I knew that I had fallen in love with Jack.

That with love, time was relative and had no specific requirements.

44

JACK

*A*s I waited for our muffins, I watched Bella waiting at our table.

A middle-aged couple, bringing a flurry of cold air with them, came in to place their order. I was surprised that so many people came out in this weather, especially so early in the morning. But I supposed they were used to it.

If I was from here, I would probably be one of those older people who moved south. Florida maybe. I liked it here, but I was glad that I was from Houston.

I could enjoy the cold weather... the snow... but I could return to Houston. I had a condo there.

Bella pulled her phone out of her pocket and started scrolling.

She would fit in anywhere. Here. Pittsburgh. Houston.

If I decided to stay here, and I could, I would be giving up a life in Houston.

Whichever one of those I decided, I would be giving her up.

She had a life in Pittsburgh.

It would be wrong to ask her to give that up.

Wouldn't it?

"Here you go," the server said, handing me a bag. I grabbed some napkins and headed back over to our table.

Bella looked up. She was looking at me as though she was trying to solve the most difficult equation imaginable.

"You okay?" I asked, sitting down and pulling the muffins out of the bag. Slid one in her direction.

"I'm good," she said, but something in her voice told me there was more to her answer.

The music changed over to a song about dashing through the snow.

"I was just thinking," she added. "Growing up, I always wanted to get away from here. More than anything. But now." She shrugged. "Now I'm finding that I actually kinda like it here."

I tried to tamp down the unexpected surge of positive emotion that came with her statement, but a smile plastered itself on my lips before I caught it.

"I like it here, too."

"What about your life in Houston?" she asked. "This must be completely different."

"It is," I admitted.

It was more different than she could ever imagine. In Houston I had every convenience. From simply pressing a button to make a latte—in my condo—to having my car brought around to the front door of my building by a valet.

Taking a walk through the snow, even if there was snow, was not even a thought in the world.

I looked into her mesmerizing green eyes and fell a little bit more in love.

In truth, I had an advantage that most people did not have.

A lot of advantages. But one in particular that made my decisions a little bit less final.

I could tap out a text message on my phone and have an

airplane waiting for me at the Whiskey Springs airport within three hours. Sometimes less.

Not that I would do that to my brother unless there was a reason for such short notice.

He was in Houston right now, celebrating Christmas with our family. Normally he lived right here in Whiskey Springs. Available to fly at a moment's notice.

Our grandfather had a Phenom stationed here and my brother—the pilot—was in charge of it.

So... I could live here and not be stuck here. I could fly to Houston in the time it took to drive across the city.

To say that I had a biased perception was an understatement.

I wasn't sure why I didn't want to tell her that just yet. I didn't want do anything to change her perception of me. I didn't want to change the focus of our budding relationship.

If I told her I was a Worthington, it might somehow alter what we had. Right now I was just a doctor working with her father doing my fellowship. For a year with the option to do more.

That was it. It was simple.

If I told her about my high-rise condo in Houston and my access to private jets, that could change everything.

So I would wait. I would hold that close to my chest, for the moment at least. Until the time to tell her seemed right.

45

BELLA

*W*hen we got back home, the house was already alive with activity. The fireplace in the living room was roaring and someone had turned on Christmas music.

If I had to guess, I'd have to say it was my cousin, Maribelle. My parents never played music during the day. I didn't know why. It just wasn't something we grew up with in our household.

Maribelle was curled up, on my favorite sofa in front of the fireplace, reading.

Aunt Rebecca and Momma were in the kitchen making hashbrowns, eggs, and biscuits. They were chatting and getting along famously.

I made coffee in my coffee machine for everyone. Then made one for Jack and myself, even though we had just had coffee. I usually had a second cup about mid-morning anyway.

"Oh," Momma said, looking over at Jack, as though she had just remembered. "Daniel called. Said he was in town and asked if he could stop by."

Jack froze, his coffee mug halfway to his lips, and stared at Momma.

Momma didn't seem the least bit concerned, but whatever she had just said had Jack looking like a deer in headlights.

Aunt Rebecca said something that I didn't pay the least bit of attention to. Something about Daniel being a nice boy.

"When?" Jack asked.

"I'm not sure," Momma said, pausing in her conversation with Aunt Rebecca. "Today. I didn't get details. I just assured him that it was okay." She paused a moment, her brow furrowed. "It is okay, right? He's always welcome here."

"Of course," Jack said. Then everything just kept going like nothing had happened.

Daddy came out of his office and looked around until he saw Jack. "Jack," he said, waving him over. "Can I borrow you for a minute?"

"Sorry," Jack said, putting a hand on my arm and stepping past me, taking his coffee with him. It would be more than a minute and we both knew it.

"No need to apologize," I said. "I know how it is." I smiled, but he seemed too preoccupied to notice.

I sat down at the kitchen table and started scrolling through my phone. I didn't need to worry about Jack. I needed to be thinking about some other things. My flight back to Pittsburgh was in two days. I was planning to leave the day after Christmas. The day after tomorrow.

Thinking about that made my heart heavy.

About thirty minutes later, the doorbell rang.

"Would you get that?" Momma asked, standing over the stove, spatula in hand.

I was already up, headed in that direction.

The doorbell rang a second time. "I'm coming already," I said, feeling irritable, though I couldn't put my finger on why.

I opened the door and automatically stepped back for

whoever it was to come inside. I assumed it was Jack's friend who had phoned to say he was stopping by. In this weather, it was important not to leave people standing in an open door. Nonetheless, a flurry of snowflakes came in with him.

"Can I take your coat?" I asked. The man's long trench coat was soaked. He obviously wasn't dressed for the weather.

"Sure," he said. "Thank you."

I took his coat as he shrugged out of it. Turned it inside out and tossed it over my arm. Beneath his coat, the man was wearing a pilot's uniform with a red Skye Travels logo on his charcoal gray jacket over a white button-down shirt.

Then I saw his name just below it. *Daniel Fleming.*

Fleming?

All I could think about was JACK *Fleming*.

I replayed the conversation from earlier. My mother seemed to know who Daniel Fleming was.

Was this the pilot who had flown my aunt and cousin in last night? I like to think I was fairly swift on my feet, dealing with college students like I did, I had to be.

But… for some reason I was having trouble wrapping my head around this particular scenario.

Jack and I hadn't talked much about his family. Just that there were a lot of them.

"You're a pilot," I blurted, not intending to speak out loud.

"Yes," he said, smiling at me. "I'm about to fly back to Houston, but I wanted to see my brother first."

Brother.

I still had my fingers wrapped around the doorknob so I braced myself against the door.

I could see a resemblance. The same lean build. The same dark hair and good looks. Similar smiling eyes. Daniel had a bigger grin, though, than Jack. At first glance, I'd say that Jack was the more serious of the two.

"He's here, right?" Daniel asked in that way that told me he'd been talking to me, but I hadn't heard him.

"Yes," I said quickly. "I'll get him."

I let go of the doorknob, pushed myself off, and went straight to the kitchen.

"Would someone tell Jack that his brother is here?" I said, then, without waiting for an answer, I headed upstairs to my bedroom.

I needed to think.

46

JACK

I stood with my older brother, Daniel, in the upstairs sitting room, overlooking my favorite morning view of the rugged Rocky Mountains.

Right now, clouds were clustered around the peaks and hanging low all around us. It was beautiful and it was deadly.

"You can't fly out in weather like this," I said.

"I know. Can't go up to Daniels House either," he said, referring to his fiancé's family home up the mountain. He was right. The road was far too dangerous in this kind of weather.

"You'll stay here," I said. "Until you can fly out."

"Thanks," he said, but I could tell he was distracted.

Rightly so. It was Christmas Eve and he wanted to spend it with his fiancé. Not stuck here in Whiskey Springs, with or without his brother.

When I'd come through the kitchen, Bella had been nowhere to be found.

I wanted to introduce them, whether it sped up the disclosure of my family's identity to her or not. At some point, my hand was going to be forced. And probably the sooner the better.

I wasn't doing a very good job of sticking to my resolution of telling her the truth. Most people considered leaving things out lying.

Wasn't sure I completely agreed, but at any rate, I didn't know where she had gotten off to.

"Who are all those people downstairs?" Daniel asked.

"Doc's sister and her daughter are here."

"Oh." He shrugged, obviously knowing nothing about the story.

"Doc's daughter is here, too."

"Bella?" Daniel asked with surprise.

"Yeah. How did you know?"

"Well, she's got a stocking hanging over the fireplace. Everyone knows she hasn't been home for years."

"She's home now," I said. For some reason, his off-handed comment irritated me. There was something judgmental in his tone.

People who didn't know the whole story, should not be allowed to make judgments. My brother included.

"Do you know why she's here?" he persisted.

"Does she need a reason?" I asked, testily.

Daniel turned and looked at me like I'd suddenly sprouted another head.

"No," he said. "I don't suppose she does."

I stared out and sipped my coffee. It wasn't objectively as good as the coffee from the coffee shop, but it tasted better simply because Bella had made it.

I took a deep breath and forced myself to take a breath.

Turning, I looked at my brother.

"How soon after you met her did you know that Jenna was the one you wanted to marry?"

Daniel blinked at me a moment, as though trying to figure out why I would ask him such a thing. He didn't even have to say it. I saw it on his face. But then he answered me.

"I knew it the moment I saw her," he said.
I sighed. Nodded a little.
"That's what I was afraid of," I said.

47

BELLA

I paced from one end of my bedroom to the other. Then stopped at the window and pressed my palms against the cool wood of the window ledge.

No one was going anywhere tonight. The storm had finally gotten here, settling in, at least, for the night.

On Christmas Eve.

The wind howled around my corner room, not bad, but it didn't take much. This corner of the house was quite sensitive to weather changes.

The snow fell steady, like flakes of raindrops, dropping a pristine blanket over everything.

I leaned forward, pressing my forehead against the cold glass, watching my breath make a little foggy spot on the window. Then I backed up and gazed out again, not looking at anything in particular, just trying to get my thoughts to settle.

Fluttering to a stop, a bright red cardinal landed on the window ledge just below me and sat there, looking up at me with brown eyes rimmed with black rings. His red feathers contrasted against the white snowfall that did not touch him.

He was uncannily close. I held perfectly still so as not to frighten him.

As we stared at each other, my mind raced, remembering the cardinal in Pittsburgh that had started this whole adventure.

Was this another sign?

The last time I had seen a cardinal at my window I had ended up here.

My phone chimed, telling me I had a text message.

The cardinal—surely he hadn't heard my phone—flew off in a flutter of wings.

I went to the nightstand and, pulling my phone off the charger, checked my messages.

I sat down hard on the bed as I stared at the name of the sender.

Antionette.

Antionette?

I hadn't heard from her since graduate school. Maybe one time. I didn't even know I still had her phone number in my phone.

ANTIONETTE RICHARDS: *Hello Bella. I hope this is still your number. It's Antionette from grad school.*

What could Antionette possibly want with me? It had been, what, four years since I'd heard from her.

I stared at the phone for maybe a full minute before it occurred to me to write her back to find out.

ME: Hi. It's still my number. Are you okay?

I watched the thought bubbles. I couldn't imagine what Antionette could possibly want with me. She and I had been a team throughout graduate school. It had been the two of us and four guys in our class. We'd kicked their ass in all our classes.

ANTIONETTE RICHARDS: *So glad. Merry Christmas!*
ME: *Merry Christmas.*

I stood up and walked back to the window, taking my cell with me. I guess I'd thought since it was Christmas Eve that she might have some magical news.

ANTIONETTE RICHARDS: *Are you still teaching?*

ME: *Yes. Same place.*

ANTIONETTE RICHARDS: *Ok. Well, something has come up. I know it's crazy, but I thought of you first. I always do. LOL.*

ME: *Sounds intriguing.*

ANTIONETTE RICHARDS: *So... I'm six months pregnant...*

ME: *OMG. Congratulations! That is.... just... so OMG.*

I walked to the other window that overlooked the road. An old car lumbered along, fighting against the snow.

ANTIONETTE RICHARDS: *Thanks. So I was about to become a stay at home mom when I came across a job posting for an online teaching position.*

ME: *Wow.*

ANTIONETTE RICHARDS: *I know, right? But they have it set up on the buddy system.*

The buddy system? What new strange idea was this?

ME: *What does that mean?*

ANTIONETTE RICHARDS: *Well... since it's all online, they prefer to have two professors paired up. For support and whatnot.*

ME: *I don't really understand what that means.*

ANTIONETTE RICHARDS: *I didn't either. But it makes a lot of sense. Working online can be lonely. I guess it would sort of like how we paired up in grad school on our projects.*

ME: *Coteaching?*

ANTIONETTE RICHARDS: *No. Just daily check ins. Sort of like a virtual water cooler. Zoom meetings, I think.*

ME: *Where do you have to live?*

ANTIONETTE RICHARDS: *That's the thing.*

I could hear the excitement in her text message, if that was even possible. I walked back to the bed and sat down again.

ANTIONETTE RICHARDS: *You can live anywhere!*

I stared at the message. *Anywhere. Anywhere?*

ME: *What do you mean?*

ANTIONETTE RICHARDS: *I know! Anywhere! It's all online. And I need a buddy. They like to hire two people together and asked if knew anyone.*

I stared outside at the snowflakes quietly falling. The rugged snowcapped mountain peaks in the distance stood sentinel over the valley.

It was so incredibly beautiful.

I swallowed thickly, my heart swelling at least three times larger… like the Grinch.

Jack. I needed to talk to Jack.

ANTIONETTE RICHARDS: *Are you still there?*

ME: *Yes! I am here. Is this a convenient time for you to call me?*

48

JACK

*D*aniel and I went for a walk in the snow. What could I say? We were from Houston and snow on Christmas Eve was a novelty to be enjoyed.

I didn't know where Bella had gone, but her mother assured me that she had gone up to her room. Not to worry.

The blue spruce trees along the side of the road were covered in fresh snowfall. Nature's way of decorating for Christmas. And the cold snow somehow brought out the fresh spruce scent.

We headed out automatically toward the coffee shop.

The streets were crowded with last-minute shoppers and people like us just out walking around enjoying the day.

"Is there something you want to tell me?" Daniel asked.

I looked over at my older brother. I was about as close to him as I was to my other siblings. There were five of us altogether. A sister between us.

"It's too early," I said.

Daniel removed his sunshades and looked at me sideways. "So there is something."

"Let's get a coffee," I said, pushing the door to the

coffeeshop open without waiting for a response. Anything to stall answering his question.

There was festivity in the air. Twinkling Christmas tree lights. Music in the background. The scent of peppermint mocha coffee.

There were only two people ahead of us—both young people, probably high school.

In line, Daniel stared at me, not letting me go without an answer.

"It's Bella," he decided, giving up on me responding, then breaking in to a wide grin.

I glared at him. "Stop it."

"When's the wedding?"

"Don't you want to meet her first?" I asked, but I couldn't keep the grin off my face, so I turned away.

"Waiting on you," he said, tapping me on the arm with his fist.

We ordered our coffee and found a table next to the window.

Daniel was already running ahead.

"You'll be living practically next door to me."

"You're kinda jumping ahead," I said.

Daniel just grinned. "So you say."

I decided it was time to steer the conversation away from me.

"Sorry you're going to miss out spending Christmas with Jenna."

Daniel shrugged. "I'm flying out tomorrow. In the morning."

I gazed out at the snow falling heavily. "Feeling a bit sure of yourself, aren't you?"

"The Phenom has superpowers."

I just stared at him.

"You're too serious, Bro."

"So you say."

"No. Seriously. It can deice itself."

I just looked blankly at him. Didn't bother to remind him that there was the matter of the runway. Was that heated, too?

"Want some advice?" Daniel asked, staring me straight in the eyes, before I could ask him for further details about the airplane. And I knew I was going to get his advice whether I wanted it or not.

"Why not?"

"Christmas Eve is the most magical day of the year. Take advantage of it."

I sipped my caramel coffee and silently agreed with him.

It wasn't just that it was Christmas Eve, it was that I was running out of time before Bella went back to Pittsburgh and I lost my chance.

But he was right. Out of all the days of the year, Christmas Eve was the one day that held true magic.

49

BELLA

*A*n hour later, my career trajectory on a completely different route, I ran downstairs to find Jack.

Everyone—Momma, Daddy, Aunt Rebecca, and Maribelle— were all sitting in the living room, sharing a bottle of wine.

I didn't have time to worry about what they were doing.

I felt so alive with excitement, I could barely contain myself.

"Has anyone seen Jack?" I asked, stopping briefly at the door, one hand on the casing.

Momma and Aunt Rebecca exchanged a glance.

"They went for a walk?" Momma said.

"Where?" Oh. Never mind. They wouldn't know anyway. I didn't wait for an answer. Just turned around, going straight to the back door, donned my gray woolen coat, looped my scarf— Jack's soft scarf—around my neck, and tugged on my gloves.

They could not have gone far. Downtown, no doubt. Where else in Whiskey Springs could they possibly go?

The snow was falling fast now. Like confetti on New Year's Eve in Times Square. But, fortunately, the sidewalks weren't slippery.

I barely noticed the fragrant blue spruce trees, delicately decorated by little stacks of snow among the branches.

A couple of chipmunks skittered across the path in front of me. I put my head down and kept walking.

As I turned left and approached Main Street, I could see the thousands—millions—of colorful twinkling lights ahead. That and the festive music filling the air.

Within minutes, I could see the coffee shop door up ahead.

I slowed down as the door opened.

As the two brothers stepped out onto the sidewalk, my heart tripped over itself and lodged itself in my throat.

They were handsome individually, but together, they looked like they could do anything.

Daniel saw me first. Nudged Jack in the ribs.

Jack scowled at him, then followed Daniel's gaze to mine.

I don't know who moved first. Maybe we moved at the same time together, meeting in halfway. But merely seconds later, I was in his arms.

"I need to talk to you." We both said it at the same time.

With a little laugh, Jack took my hand and led me back toward the coffee shop.

"Daniel," he said as we walked past his brother. "This is Bella."

"We met," Daniel said, a little grin on his face.

Then before there could be any other conversation, Jack practically dragged me through the doors into the coffee shop.

No one paid us any mind as he led me to an empty table next to the sparkling, twinkling Christmas tree. We sat across from each other. I shivered, still too cold to take my coat off.

"You need to talk to me?" I needed to know, but I was afraid of his answer. Anything could have happened now that his brother was here.

"Yes," he said, leaning forward and taking both my hands in his. "I just need to tell you what I'm thinking."

"Okay," I said, watching him carefully, looking for any clue of what he was thinking.

He rubbed my gloved thumb with his. "I like it here. A lot."

"I do, too."

He kept talking. "My brother Daniel is going to be making his home here. At the Daniels House."

That sounded like a conversation for another time, so I just nodded that I'd heard him.

"I'm thinking maybe I'll want to take over your father's practice. After I complete my fellowship, of course. He's just made me a very generous offer."

"I see. Congratulations." So that was what their meeting had been about.

"Anyway... That's not what I wanted to talk to you about exactly." He was nervous. I could see it in his eyes. "I know you live in Pittsburgh. But do you think we could work together to try to figure out a way to make this work?"

When I didn't answer, he brought one of my hands to his lips and placed a kiss on my bare wrist just below my glove.

It sent a delicious shiver through me.

"Okay," I said.

He looked at me as though he'd expected a completely different answer. "Okay?"

"Yes." I smiled. "I'd like that."

He looked surprised and relieved all at once. He gazed into my eyes.

"I don't want to be apart from you."

I smiled. "I think I know how we can work it out."

"Really?" He apparently seemed to expect opposition.

"Really." I nodded.

"But..." He sat back, looking at me like he was waiting for the other shoe to drop.

"But... yes... I like teaching college. And no... I never thought I'd move back here."

"But…"

I grinned. "But." I looked around at the little coffee shop. Right in the middle of the little town I had fought for years to get away from and to stay away from.

But, it turns out I had been fighting for the wrong reasons.

This wasn't the place I needed to try to get away from. This was the place I needed to get back to.

The Christmas music blended with the voices of people who belonged here and it was only now, in this moment, that I realized I belonged here.

But only with Jack. Without Jack there would have no purpose for me to be here. For me they were a package deal. Apart, they were one thing, but together, they were synergistically perfect.

"If you're serious about all that," I said, fighting sudden moisture threatening to spill from my eyes.

"I'm serious." He said the words without the least bit of hesitation, even before I got the last word of my sentence out.

"Then… yes."

"Yes?"

"Yes. I'll stay in Whiskey Springs with you."

He looked right at me, his gaze locked onto mine, but I couldn't read his expression. He looked like he wanted to believe me, but didn't dare.

"Just like that?"

"Just like that."

"How?"

I gazed into his deep, sparkling blue eyes. "I honestly don't know how it happened."

Without warning, before I knew what he was doing, he pulled me to him, to sit in his lap, wrapping his arms around me.

I looked around, automatically worrying about what people thought, but no one was watching us. No one cared.

"I know how," he said.

"How?" I asked, looking at him with skepticism and even more so, amusement.

"It's the magic of Christmas Eve."

I remembered the cardinal that had visited my window before I got the text from Antoinette. A cardinal at Christmas was said to be an omen of good things to come.

And now I was a believer.

If anyone ever asked me how Jack and I met, I'd tell them the cardinal brought us together.

Then he kissed me.

And I fell head long into the magic of Whiskey Springs.

EPILOGUE
BELLA

One Year Later

"What does this do?" I asked, pressing a button on the console next to my seat before Jack had time to answer.

As far as airplanes went, it was quiet, a steady roar in the background.

A little screen dropped out of the ceiling of the Phenom 100 private jet.

Jack was watching me with an amused expression.

We'd flown before, of course, but this was the first time we'd flown in one of the Phenoms—a Skye Travels top of the line private jet.

The airplane interior was in piano black—black leather seats with white walls. There was room for four passengers—maybe seven according to Jack—but right now it only held two passengers. Me and Jack.

Jack and I sat next to each other, fastened in four-point harnesses. Skye Travels had two main priorities. Safety and customer satisfaction.

Jack pressed a button on his side and an image of our route appeared on the screen.

"Looks like we'll be in Whiskey Springs before lunch."

"That's perfect," I said. "After lunch Momma wants us to help her decorate the tree."

Jack rolled his eyes, but I knew it was a token protest.

"What's her theme this year?" he asked.

"I'm not sure," I said with a little frown as I remembered last year's bird theme. We'd only taken honorable mention—fourth place out of twelve. I pulled out my phone, intending to show him a picture that Momma had sent me, but I quickly discovered that we had Internet.

"We have Internet." I looked over at him, but I could tell by his expression that he already knew this.

I shrugged and quickly found the picture Momma had sent me. It was a sketch—one she had apparently done herself. Momma, unfortunately, was not an artist.

Holding up my phone, I stretched my arm out across the aisle for Jack to see.

He pressed a button on his own console and his chair slid over next to mine.

"How did you do that?" I asked, looking down at my own chair.

"I have so much to teach you," he said.

I made a sound that could be interpreted into whatever he wanted.

"Let me see this… sketch," he said, looking at the photo on my phone. "Your mother is not an artist," he said.

"I know. But whatever it is, we can make it work. Maybe we'll get more than honorable mention this year."

He zoomed in on the photo, then looked at me sideways.

"You know what this is, don't you?" he asked.

"I didn't look at it in too much detail." In truth, I'd barely looked at it. It was much too difficult to figure out so I decided to simply wait until we got to the high school gym to see the decorations in person.

"It's a wedding theme." He looked at me with an unreadable expression.

"Surely not," I said, peering over at the sketch.

"Look," he said. "There's a little wedding cake."

I put a hand over my mouth to hide my surprise.

"My mother isn't very subtle, is she?"

"Subtlety is not her strong point," he said, looking at other parts of the sketch.

"Well, we don't have to wonder what she's thinking."

We flew through a bank of fluffy white clouds. The fasten seatbelt light flashed on. We were already firmly belted in.

"It's probably all about my upcoming brother's wedding." Charlie's wedding date was June 15. My brother had taken his time, but I would bet money that it wasn't his idea to wait. He was already living with his fiancé Jenna Garrison up at the Daniels House.

"Maybe," Jack said, absently, handing my phone back to me.

"Maybe not?" I tucked the phone back into my bag.

"You know it's a maybe not. Your mother doesn't have much patience."

"She's been really patient with Charlie."

"True. But a mother can have only so much patience for these things." He linked his fingers with mine.

"How do you know that?"

"Have you already forgotten meeting all my family? With that many aunts, a guy couldn't help but know how the female mind works."

I narrowed my eyes at him. He said that, but... I wasn't so sure just whether he really knew or just thought he knew. And he may say he knew how women thought, but I wasn't so sure if he knew how I thought.

I caught my breath as we hit a pocket of turbulence. Jack

didn't even seem to notice. Perhaps it was because he'd spent so much time in the air with the pilots in his family. Grandfather. Uncles. Cousins. Even aunts.

I was beginning to think that flying for him wasn't much different from riding in a car for most people.

He swore, however, that he had absolutely no knowledge of how to actually fly a plane. I didn't believe him. Not completely anyway.

In the year that I'd known him, I'd found that he knew a little bit about just about everything. And if he didn't know, he looked it up.

"There's no time like the present," he muttered.

"What?"

I grabbed his hand when we hit another pocket of turbulence.

"Hold on a minute," he said, pulling his cell out of his coat pocket and sending a text.

He received a response almost immediately.

"Who's that?" I asked, thinking it might have something to do with the airplane and the turbulence.

"The pilot."

"Why? What's wrong?" I wasn't a particularly nervous flyer. I thought of myself as more of a cautious flyer. But I could admit that turbulence, especially in this small plane made me nervous.

"Wait ten minutes," Jack said.

"For what?"

"Just wait." He demonstrated what he wanted me to do by leaning his head back on the seat and closing his eyes.

I blew out of breath of frustration and pulled the novel I was reading from my handbag. Then I proceeded to read. I read the same sentence five times before giving up. I closed the book and dropped it back into my handbag.

What was the deal with ten minutes anyway?

I forced myself to relax. Jack always had a reason for what could be construed as insanity.

After what must have been ten minutes, the plane burst out of the clouds and back into blue sky.

Jack got another text.

He released his seatbelt harness.

"What are you doing?" I asked, with alarm.

"We're out of the turbulence," he said.

"But—"

Before I could figure out my question, Jack was on his knees.

"What—?"

"Bella," he said, looking into my eyes. "I was going to wait until we got to Whiskey Springs, but it just seems like something I need to go ahead and do before we get surrounded by people."

My heart raced as I just looked blankly at him. I didn't know what he was doing, but I did know what it usually meant when a guy got down on one knee.

But on an airplane?

"Bella," he said again.

I took a deep breath. "Jack?"

He reached into his jacket pocket and pulled out a quintessential Tiffany's blue box.

I looked from the box up into his sparkling blue eyes. Searching.

"Bella," he said again.

I opened my mouth to repeat his name, but just closed it. And waited.

"Will you marry me?"

I wanted to answer. I did. But I couldn't get my voice to work.

"Are you okay?" he asked.

"I…" I blinked rapidly, trying—not so successfully—to keep the tears from spilling over.

"Please tell me those are happy tears," he said, setting the box on his seat and taking both of my hands in his.

I nodded. "Yes. Happy." I swallowed thickly and looked over at the box questioningly.

He released my hands and, picking up the box, opened it to reveal a sparkly diamond engagement ring.

"Yes," I said, finding my voice.

He pulled the ring out and placed it on my finger.

"I love you," he said. "You'll marry me?"

"Yes," I said, struggling unsuccessfully with my seatbelt latch.

He reached over, unhooked it easily, and then I was in his arms.

To say that I was on the top of the world, was not just a literal statement.

I was truly on top of the world in every way possible.

My heart was bursting with happiness.

And then he kissed me.

Keep Reading for a preview of DRAGON'S BLOOD…

PREVIEW DRAGON'S BLOOD

Chapter 1
Reed Smith

I stood on the street corner of Main Street and Alexander Avenue in the little mountain town of Whiskey Springs, Colorado and watched tourists crossing the streets like sheep. Families. Young couples. Older couples. A few people walking by themselves.

They followed the rules. For the most part.

Waited at the street corners for the green hand signals giving them the go ahead to cross the street.

The sun was warm on my head, bare except for my short dark brown hair, military haircut, but the breeze coming off the mountains had a chill to it. Even on a hot day in the middle of July, the heat was tempered by a coolness coming off the snowcapped mountains.

I stood in place, like a statue at attention. I wore dark

shades over my eyes. It felt odd to be out in public wearing blue jeans, a polo shirt, and white canvas sneakers. All new.

My feet glued to the sidewalk, I let people walk around me. It earned me more than a few curious and even more irritated glances.

The traffic lights turned red and the vehicles took their turn. Bumper to bumper. Tourists driving here and there. Into the national park for the day. Shopping. Some just driving through, out for a drive.

Then there were the locals. In a hurry to get where they were going. Mostly annoyed with the tourists, but most had sense enough not to show it. Without the tourists, the town would dry up into a ghost town.

Music blaring from one of the passing cars was followed by the loud beep of a horn.

It was funny. City people came out here to get away from the city, yet they brought the city with them. The sounds. The crowds. The impatience.

They didn't even realize it.

As the crossing light turned back to green, a couple of teenagers decided to break the rules and take a short cut. Dressed in shorts and brand new bright red Rocky Mountain National Park t-shirts, they headed across the street at a diagonal. Jaywalking.

The cop's shrill whistle stopped everyone in their tracks long enough to see that they weren't the ones in trouble. Everyone except the two teens. They laughed and started running.

My muscles tensed with instinct to go after the two boys. But it was not my job.

Retired.

The word still felt gritty in my mouth.

Retired at thirty-two.

Four years of college—ROTC followed by ten years in the Air Force.

New President. New rules. New orders.

And just like that the military was done with me.

Honorable discharge and all that. Full benefits befitting the officer I was. Had been.

Didn't matter. My plan had been to be career military.

Just like my father.

But my father's purple heart had come posthumously.

I'd always known that no matter how hard I tried, I would never match my father's success. He had been a hero in my eyes.

But I'd always had a chance. As long as I was active military, there had been a chance. Now I was on the street. A civilian.

People walked around me through the next round of lights. More dirty looks.

The policeman stopped the two boys who had the decency to lower their gazes as he handed them a citation.

Good. Law and order at work.

I was a firm believer in law and order.

The boys had to learn early or they would never respect authority.

My father had taught me early and it had served me well.

Tired of getting dirty looks, I turned away from the intersection and ambled, hands in my pockets, down the sidewalk. Hands in the pockets seemed like breaking a rule. I did it intentionally. To try and blend in.

I passed a bookstore displaying the latest bestseller. Not too many people hitting the bookstore today. With all the digital books, I rarely saw anyone holding an actual paper book anymore.

I guess I was the exception. I liked the feel of a book in my hands. The turning of the page. The special bookmark my sister had given me as a Christmas gift. It was faded and tattered now, but I used it anyway.

I kept walking. Today I was not in the market for anything to read. I had a science fiction novel in my overnight bag.

The next shop was a ski shop. Empty. Not much business in the summer for a ski shop. Maybe they sold other things. I didn't stop in to see.

But I stopped at the next door. Considered. Then stepped inside.

Perfect.

It was half café. Half bar. The owner was smart, serving burgers and fries as well as beer and whiskey.

Cool. Dark. Quiet. The television over the bar broadcast a baseball game, but the volume was turned down to barely audible.

There were a dozen tables, half of them booths along the windows. The bar was on the back wall with a full mahogany top worn with age. Lots of dings, but still shiny. A large stone hearth fireplace, tall enough for a man to stand up in, was on the wall to the right.

Not empty, but not crowded.

Half a dozen people sitting here and there. A middle-aged couple sitting at a booth having a hamburger. The other customers sitting at the bar.

"Welcome to Whiskey Springs Saloon," the man behind the bar said. Slightly overweight, he sported a bushy beard and a full-neck tattoo.

"Thanks." I slid onto the nearest bar stool and tucked my shades into my collar. "Can I get a bottle of Mill—?"

The bartender slid a cold bottle of Miller Lite across the worn mahogany bar.

"Lite," I finished my sentence.

Odd coincidence. Maybe everyone ordered a Miller Lite.

"No problem," the bartender said. "Can I get you anything else?"

The bartender had a flat affect. No smile. No emotion. But he sounded friendly enough.

"I'll let you know," I said, lifting my bottle to him and taking a sip. The beer was icy cold. Just the way I liked it. My men had always ribbed me about my aversion to warm beer.

A man liked what he liked.

With a shrug, the bartender slung a white cloth over his shoulder and straightened the already perfectly spaced glasses hanging above the bar. Apparently not all the customers drank beer out of a bottle.

In fact, there was only one other fellow at the other end of the bar drinking beer. The others had glasses of what looked like whiskey.

Refusing to add it to my list of worries, I stretched out my legs and made myself comfortable.

I'd found my way here, presumably to think.

So think I would do.

My parents had brought me and my sister here every summer for a month-long vacation. A three-bedroom cabin on the river. As far as I could remember, it was always the same cabin. They must have had a standing reservation. It had only been one month out of the year, but it was the one constant in my life. We'd moved around a lot during the year as my father was stationed at one base, then another.

But every year we came back to this one little town. Until we didn't.

I was sixteen when it happened. My wounded father was flown to Germany and given the best medical care in the world. But he did not come home.

My mother and her two children stayed in Alabama where Father had left her. And we never returned to Colorado as a family. I had never come back either.

Until today.

A vacation spot should never be the one constant place in a child's life.

But in some odd way, this was home to me.

I ran my fingers along the smooth wood of the bar.

My life could turn now. Go in a completely different direction.

I'd never married or had children because I did not want to subject them to the military life I had grown up in.

But now…

I wasn't sure I was ready to do anything drastic.

I needed time to think.

To just be.

To get my bearings.

I did not have to hurry. The military was taking care of me, financially at least. I guess that was some consolation.

The grandfather clock standing next to the stairs leading to the second floor chimed the hour.

Chapter 2
Andrea Auclair

1866

I SAT at the vanity in my room and fussed with my hair.

I'd brushed it one hundred strokes just like my mother had taught me as a little girl. I might be twenty-one now, but it was one of those things that was ingrained in my system. Besides, most nights I found it soothing. Not tonight though.

Tonight I was nervous. I had no reason to be nervous. This was just a business deal. Not worthy of this level of worry. If this didn't work out, something else would.

I was just so weary of traveling. I wanted to just be somewhere. To be settled.

Breaking the silence, a horse and wagon traveled along the dirt road beneath my second-floor window. There was never much traffic in the small town. One of the things I liked about it.

Somewhere in the distance I heard a blacksmith's hammer banging against iron. Fashioning a horseshoe perhaps. So strange that horses wore shoes.

If I listened really hard, I could hear the strains of piano music drifting from the saloon. Someone was always playing the only piano in town.

A lot of the ladies here in town were from the south where learning to play the piano was a normal part of their upbringing. Just as it had been mine.

I had been in the saloon one time. Although it was overall what I had expected of a saloon in appearance, it felt more like a café with a bar in it. It had a wall of glass windows with a picturesque view of the Rocky Mountains.

Sitting here in my room, if I turned to my right, I could see the peaks of the mountains in the distance. It was full on summer and they still had snow on them.

Since I'd never seen snow, I could not fathom how snow could be there in the middle of summer.

Just one of the many wonders of this place I hoped to call home.

I wove a blue ribbon that matched my high-collared dress through my hair and tied it into a bow behind my ear.

Not exactly the look I was going for, but it would do.

The cook was downstairs, preparing supper. Even up here, the scent of biscuits and gravy was strong enough to make my mouth water. We had not had much to eat on the long trip from New Orleans to Colorado. A lot of beans and stale biscuits. When there was meat, no one asked what kind it was. If we knew, it was doubtful we would have been able to eat it.

Twirling around on the bench, my clean muslin skirts rustling with the movement, I looked across the room at the supplies we had carted in the bottom of the wagon all the way from New Orleans. A stack of blank paint canvases tied together with a strand of rope. A box of paints and brushes and a box of charcoals.

It wasn't much to anyone else, but to my sister, it was of utmost importance.

I was certain Bailey was ready to spread them out somewhere and capture the wonderful things we were seeing. To do more than the few charcoal sketches she had done during our travels. But there had been so very much to do for the last few months.

It had taken all hands on deck. With me being the oldest of five children, each spaced one year apart, I had quickly learned to be even more responsible than I had been before.

When Father had gone off to fight in the war, he had left Mother in charge of their huge family. That had been five years ago.

Then mother had succumbed to a bout of yellow fever only a few months ago. I still felt like I was walking around in a fog. Still could not believe that both our parents were gone.

Next in line after our parents to take care of us was our uncle. Uncle Pete, never married, turned out to be not only a scoundrel, but also a gambler. He had gambled away our home. Fortunately, he had not had access to money in our parents' bank account, so I had that.

With my four younger siblings in tow, I had taken the money from the bank and the money our mother had squirreled away herself and essentially vanished into the night.

West.

Before the war, my father had often talked of going west.

He knew nothing more of the west than what he learned from the dime novels he voraciously read, but it did not matter.

His dream had been passed on to me.

Not that it was my dream, necessarily, but maybe he had somehow made it my destiny.

Destiny was a slippery thing. Hard to hold, bouncing in what looked like a random fashion from place to place.

But I was certain it was far from random.

My father had shaped me. There was a reason he had told me stories of the west before I could even read. Planted those images in my head.

He had made me who I was. And my mother had made me responsible for my siblings.

Those two things swirled together inside me making me who I was.

So here we were. In the small town of Whiskey Springs, Colorado Territory.

With no idea of what would come next.

Whatever it was, I would handle it. My siblings and I had come this far. I told myself it would be an adventure.

Patting my cheeks and forcing a smile onto my lips, I prepared to face what surely must be the next chapter in our lives.

Keep Reading DRAGON'S BLOOD...

Kathryn Kaleigh is the author of over seventy novels, over one hundred short stories, and many collections.

kathrynkaleigh.com

www.ingramcontent.com/pod-product-compliance
Lightning Source LLC
Chambersburg PA
CBHW020640130726
47903CB00003BA/849